THE ART OF PICKING UP GIRLS

THE ART OF PICKING UP GIRLS

(and other dangerous things)

ERIC WALTERS

razor bill

RAZORBILL
an imprint of Penguin Canada Books Inc., a Penguin Random House Company

Published by the Penguin Group
Penguin Canada Books Inc., 320 Front Street West, Suite 1400, Toronto, Ontario M5V 3B6, Canada

Penguin Group (USA) LLC, 375 Hudson Street, New York, New York 10014, U.S.A.
Penguin Books Ltd, 80 Strand, London WC2R 0RL, England
Penguin Ireland, 25 St Stephen's Green, Dublin 2, Ireland (a division of Penguin Books Ltd)
Penguin Group (Australia), 707 Collins Street, Melbourne, Victoria 3008, Australia (a division of Pearson Australia Group Pty Ltd)
Penguin Books India Pvt Ltd, 11 Community Centre, Panchsheel Park, New Delhi – 110 017, India
Penguin Group (NZ), 67 Apollo Drive, Rosedale, Auckland 0632, New Zealand
(a division of Pearson New Zealand Ltd)
Penguin Books (South Africa) (Pty) Ltd, 24 Sturdee Avenue, Rosebank, Johannesburg 2196, South Africa

Penguin Books Ltd, Registered Offices: 80 Strand, London WC2R 0RL, England

First published 2016

1 2 3 4 5 6 7 8 9 10 (RRD)

Copyright © Eric Walters, 2016

Publisher's note: This book is a work of fiction. Names, characters, places and incidents either are the product of the author's imagination or are used fictitiously, and any resemblance to actual persons living or dead, events, or locales is entirely coincidental.

Manufactured in the U.S.A.

LIBRARY AND ARCHIVES CANADA CATALOGUING IN PUBLICATION

Walters, Eric, 1957-, author
      The art of picking up girls (and other dangerous things) / Eric Walters.

Issued in print and electronic formats.
ISBN 978-0-14-319497-2 (paperback).--ISBN 978-0-14-319499-6 (epub)

      I. Title.

PS8595.A598A68 2016   jC813'.54   C2015-907165-8
                                                 C2015-907166-6

Visit the Penguin Canada website at **www.penguinrandomhouse.ca**

For all those who know that no matter what the question,
love is the answer. And for Anita — my answer.

CHAPTER ONE

"Are you Fox, first name Graham?"

I looked up from my lunch. There was a guy standing there. I didn't know him. Big shock. I didn't know anybody in the whole cafeteria, in the whole school, in the whole city. What made it even worse was starting three weeks into the school year, when everybody else had already started to find their place.

"Yeah?" I asked, feeling at least a little suspicious.

"I'm Frost, first name Ethan. Can I sit down?"

I motioned to a chair and he pulled it out, swung it around, and straddled it. He looked like he was about my age, probably a senior. He was the type of guy who prided himself on how he dressed, how his hair looked—he had that air of confidence, almost arrogance. I knew the type. At my old school, some people probably thought I *was* that type.

It was my first week at this new school, and I'd almost got used to sitting by myself. It was the first time I'd ever been the new guy in a school in my life. We'd moved here from Woodstock, the small town I was born in. Sitting here by myself was strange, but I wasn't sure I had the energy to make new friends. It was my senior year—what was the point of getting to know anyone when we were all just going to graduate and leave? At least, that's what I'd been telling myself.

Ethan looked at me as if sizing me up. It was a little uncomfortable, but on the other hand, it felt good to have somebody sitting at the table with me. I'd never thought of myself as being self-conscious or uncomfortable being on my own. Of course, before this I'd never been on my own. I'd always had Elmer, my best friend—correction, *former* best friend— beside me. But now, sitting alone all week as a stream of strangers went by, I had started feeling like I was on display. Exhibit A: the boy without friends.

"So Fox, first name Graham, you must be wondering why I'm here."

"I was, Frost, first name Ethan."

He chuckled. "I am your official guide."

"Shouldn't you have been here on Monday when I started?"

"A few days ago this wasn't something I even dreamed I'd have to do. Now I'm your host, your new, and, judging from the crowd at this table, your *only* friend at this school." He offered his hand and I reluctantly shook it. I wasn't so sure I wanted a guide—or a friend.

"So you must also be wondering why somebody as obviously cool and attractive as I am is doing a job they generally give to bottom-feeders."

I tried not to react to that statement. I had been a host for a couple of new students at my old school and I was no bottom-feeder. I'd been vice-president of the student council, played on the football and basketball teams, and I'd had lots of friends.

"I see you are speechless, so I'll answer my own question. You are one incredibly lucky individual," he said.

I laughed. "Yeah, that's exactly how I've been feeling, really lucky. I'm in a new school where I know nobody, in a new city where I know nobody. 'Lucky' is just the word I'd use."

"You *weren't* lucky. Now you are! I will bring you luck by providing you with genuine, real advice, as opposed to the usual where-is-the-washroom, guiding you to classes sort of help that hosts usually offer. You will be very grateful for the wisdom I will impart to you."

"It would be good to know where the washrooms are, actually."

"Female, male, or staff?" he asked.

"Let's start with male and work our way through the others in time."

"I like that. So far you have not been the disappointment I expected you to be."

"I'd be offended if that wasn't the nicest thing anyone's said to me today. So, what made you decide to be a host?" I asked.

"I am *your* luck. You are part of *my* punishment."

"Punishment?"

"I was offered a three-day suspension or this hosting gig."

"Glad to know I'm better than a suspension."

"A *three-day* suspension. If it had been a one-day suspension, I probably would have taken it."

"What did you do?" I asked.

"You obviously don't know about prison etiquette or you wouldn't ask me about the crime," he said.

"Sorry, I wouldn't want to be guilty of that."

"And never ask if somebody is guilty. Assume innocence, even in the face of overwhelming evidence."

"I'll try to remember that."

"You should, because mostly this is less about what I did and more about what the vice-principal calls my 'bad attitude.'"

"And do you have a bad attitude?"

"I have *an* attitude. Everybody except corpses and the walking dead has an attitude. I have no control over whether somebody thinks my attitude is good or bad. That is more about *their* attitude or perception."

"Just so I understand, the combination of you doing something wrong and a perceived bad attitude is what qualified you to be a host?" I asked.

"Makes no sense at all, does it? I assume they believe either that this hosting role will have a transforming effect on me or that you simply aren't worth worrying about."

"That's about how I feel here." I gestured around the cafeteria. "How big is this school?"

"Twenty-five hundred lost souls."

"My last school had four hundred."

"That's not a school, it's a bus stop."

"Where I'm from, the whole town of Woodstock only has ten thousand people."

"Woodstock? Never heard of it," he said.

"I'm not surprised. It's almost eight hundred miles from here."

"Do you know anybody here at all?"

"My parents and my sister—that's about it."

"Well, Small Town, now you know me, and it's like they say, it isn't *what* you know as much as *who* you know."

He reached over and grabbed a couple of fries off my plate. "So, what brings you to us partway through your senior year?" he asked through a mouthful of fries.

"My father works as an accountant for an insurance company and he got offered a big promotion, but he had to start right away."

"So it was good for him, and he didn't care what it was like for you or the rest of the family."

I almost yelled out "Yeah!" but I didn't. Finally, someone had said out loud what I was sure we had all been thinking. My sister was in eighth grade and also had to start a new school, and my mother had to resign her teaching position. She was now back to being a supply teacher. But I also knew that it had been a hard decision for my dad.

"It was too good for him to turn down. He didn't have a choice," I said.

"There are always choices, but you keep saying that if it makes it feel less like you got screwed." He grabbed a couple more of my fries.

I had got screwed. This was my senior year. It was supposed to be special. It was supposed to be the best year and—

"Look, anyway you cut it, your father got a promotion and you feel like you got a demotion," Ethan said.

That's how it *did* feel. I shrugged and nodded ever so slightly in agreement. There had even been some talk about me staying in Woodstock, living with my best friend, and finishing out the school year. Then things had changed, and that became impossible.

"But that's where you, my friend, Mr. Small Town, are wrong. Being here is not a demotion. It's an opportunity. One that I'm going to help you take full advantage of."

"Are you driving me back to Woodstock?"

"Oh, God, no, leaving Hicksville was probably the best thing that ever happened to you. How about I meet you by the main doors right after school?"

"Why?"

"As you said, you don't know anybody, so I'll take it upon myself to be the Welcome Wagon for the entire city. Unless you have something else planned."

"My calendar has been cleared off, against my will."

"Another thing we have in common."

"Hey, Frosty!"

I looked up to see three guys coming toward us. Judging from the confident way they were walking through the caf, joking around, they were the "cool kids." They had the right hair, right clothes, and right attitude—in fact, they looked like they should be friends with Ethan. All three greeted him with hand-shakes and high-fives.

"Glenn, Ashton, Cody, I'd like you to meet my new friend, Graham the Fox."

They all nodded in a friendly way. Maybe things were looking up?

"You are now friends with some of the coolest guys in the school, three-fifths of our starting five for the basketball team," Ethan said.

The three of them being basketball players didn't surprise me. They had the look, the swagger.

"I was on our school team. I played guard," I said.

"Too bad you weren't here for the tryouts," Ethan said. "Especially since we are now one guard short."

"We were almost an entire team short," Glenn said. "Frosty, I don't know how we can repay you."

"Win a lot of games. Get a scholarship. Name your first-born male children after me."

"Girl or boy, my first child is going to be called Ethan, or Frosty, one of the two."

"We all owe you," Cody added. "You took a bullet for us."

"For me it was an activity. For you, gentlemen, it's potentially a university ride and maybe a career. Wait, instead of naming your children after me, how about guaranteed seats if any of you make it to the show?"

"You got it, Frosty! You got it!" Glenn yelled out, then he suddenly looked sheepish as he glanced around. I scanned the room as well—what was he looking at, or for? The only thing I noticed was that everyone at the surrounding tables seemed to be watching us. That just confirmed that these guys were something big in the school. I hoped they'd all now see that I wasn't completely without friends.

"We'd better get going," Cody said. "You know, just in case."

"I understand," Ethan said.

"We miss you," Ashton said. "We all miss you."

"It's just not the same," Cody added, and Glenn nodded.

"Okay, now you'd all better get going before you start crying like you're playing on the girls' basketball team."

They said their goodbyes and started away, but then Glenn spun back around.

"I meant what I said. We all owe you."

"No biggie."

"Yes it was. Memory of an elephant." He tapped a finger against the side of his head and then pointed at me. "You're lucky. You have the Frostman as your friend, and things will never be boring. Hang onto your hat and enjoy the ride because it could get a little wild . . . I know that from personal experience."

They all walked away leaving me and "the Frostman" alone again. Everyone around us turned back to their lunches and the buzz of conversation grew.

"So you're the point guard they're missing?" I asked.

"I'm encouraged to see that not much gets past you."

Without asking he reached over and grabbed the other half of my sandwich. He took a bite. He made a face and dropped it back on my plate.

"That is disgusting," he said. "Who eats cafeteria food?"

"You haven't been complaining about my fries."

"Fries are fries. Even the morons in the cafeteria can't screw those up. And yes, I was a point guard, but certainly not a starter."

"And you got kicked off the team as part of your punishment."

"You are now two for two. I may have to start calling you Sherlock, Small Town."

"What exactly did you . . . wait, I'm not supposed to ask that."

"I'm sure you'll find out soon enough anyway. It's still the talk of the school. We were in a tournament out of town last weekend, and apparently there were allegations of underage drinking and some local girls joining members of the team in their hotel rooms."

"Allegations?"

"Well, they're always just allegations until proven in a court of law. Unfortunately, the school is not a court and they didn't need proof. They were going to suspend the whole team for ten games."

"Ten games? That's more than half the season. That's not a suspension, it's a death sentence," I said.

"Exactly. So I figured it was better for one person to take the fall instead of all of us."

"So you confessed?"

"Confession is for church. I just told them it was all my doing—the girls, the alcohol, everything."

"Wow, so that's what Cody meant by you taking a bullet. But he was wrong."

"What do you mean?"

"You jumped on a live grenade. That's even more impressive."

"I like the way you put that. It was like a live grenade."

"So they kicked you off the team."

"Threw me away like an old jockstrap. What I didn't know when I jumped on the grenade was that I was also going to be banned from going to games, and that the guys on the team were actually not going to be allowed to associate with me during school hours for the rest of the season."

"That's harsh." That also explained why they'd seemed so nervous talking to him in the caf, and why they didn't sit down.

"It makes the whole hosting thing even more bizarre. 'Mr. Frost, you are not to have contact with the members of the basketball team,'" he said, in a put-on voice that I had to assume was the vice-principal's. "'But we do want you to spend time with a new student, take him under your wing, and influence him.'"

"Truth is stranger than fiction," I said.

"So, now that you know my darkest secret, still want to do something after school?"

"Why not?" It sounded like this guy was a pretty good friend to have. Being my only friend would make him my best friend.

"Okay, then, it's agreed. Last bell, front steps, look for me."

He got up and sauntered away. He wasn't on the basketball team any more but he still looked like he was. As he moved, he exchanged a few words with kids at different tables. It was obvious that he had a lot more friends than just the guys on the team. He might have been down a few, but he was still in a different category than me.

"Excuse me."

I turned. It was a girl—an attractive girl. She was tall, blond, with blue eyes. She looked more than a bit like my old girlfriend, Jenn. I offered her a weak little smile. It was the best I could do.

"I couldn't help overhearing," she said. "You probably want to avoid him."

"Ethan?"

"Yeah. Do yourself a favour and find another friend, any other friend. He's the biggest *jerk* in the school."

Before I could say anything, she turned and walked away.

For a split second I thought about going after her to ask her more, but the bell rang. Lunch was over, and I had to find my period three class. I guess I should have asked my new best friend where the chemistry lab was.

CHAPTER TWO

Right after last class I made a quick stop at my locker and got to the front steps of the school as fast as I could. I'd sort of made a vow to keep to myself as much as possible, to keep some distance. Not getting involved kept you safer. But since lunch, I'd found myself looking forward to the end of the day, to actually meeting a friend. And now I was there . . . but he wasn't.

Fifteen minutes went by, and the crowd was thinning out. The longer I waited, the worse it felt. Maybe that girl was right and he was a jerk.

People passed by me, and it felt strange not to know who they were. At my old school I would have known everybody, and they would have known me. Unfortunately, at the end they would have known me as that guy who got dumped by his girlfriend, that guy whose best friend started dating her. I'd heard little comments. Some people were genuinely sad for me. Others gave me looks of pity. Some looked almost pleased by the whole thing. Here at least I got none of that. Instead it was almost like I was invisible.

Of course I'd tried to convince myself that maybe she wouldn't have dumped me if I hadn't been moving away. But maybe that was just the excuse for her to end it, and it had been coming all along. The lightning speed with which they'd hooked up after the breakup made me think that it had at least been in the planning stages. What an idiot I was. And now I was looking like an idiot again because Ethan wasn't going to show.

I started to walk down the stairs to leave, but I'd only taken a few steps when a red BMW convertible pulled up to the curb in front of the school, music blaring, the bass almost shaking the steps. It was Ethan. He saw me, waved, and yelled out, "Hey, Foxy! Come on, your ride is waiting!"

I waved back and started toward the car, taking the steps two at a time, but then slowed myself down. I didn't want to appear too relieved or too desperate. I could see people around me staring as I pulled open the car door and jumped in. Before I could grab the seatbelt, almost before I could pull the door shut, he squealed away, leaving a trail of rubber on the pavement.

"You know how to make an entrance and an exit," I said.

"What?" he screamed over the music. He turned it down.

"I said nice car."

"It's all right. My father originally tried to get me something that was made in this country, you know, buy local."

"You don't agree?"

"Cars are like wines. Domestic is almost never as good as foreign."

"I wouldn't know about foreign cars or any type of wine. I'm more of a beer guy." Although, to be truthful, I really didn't drink much of anything.

"So, where do you live?"

"Not far. It's called Hepburn; it's over in the—"

"I know where that is. I'm in a subdivision on Palm Boulevard, not far away. Do you mind if we make a stop on the way home?"

"No, of course not."

"I want to pick something up at the mall. Maybe you can pick up something too."

"I don't really need anything."

"*Need* and *want* are two very different things. What I have in mind you'll definitely want."

He laughed like he was enjoying a private joke.

"So, how are you enjoying your new world?" he asked.

"There are a lot of people, and a lot traffic."

"And, *golly gee*, some of these here buildings is almost fifteen storeys tall!" he said, putting on an accent like he was some gomer from the sticks. Was that what he thought I was?

"I've been in bigger cities than this." I tried not to sound too defensive.

"Living in is different from visiting. Just remember—

a bigger city means more opportunities, more chances to have fun."

"I'm in favour of fun."

"Are you?" he asked. "Are you talking 'fun' like having a single-scoop vanilla ice cream cone? Or 'fun' like forty flavours, sprinkles, toppings, and all you can eat until you either get a stomach ache or brain freeze?"

"I don't like vanilla."

"Good to hear, because I don't *do* vanilla, or single-scoop."

He turned into a parking lot.

"Wow, a mall, how *fun*," I said sarcastically. "Are we really going for an ice cream cone?"

"We're going to be picking up the flavour of the day, and in here there'll be even more than forty to pick from," he replied.

He pulled into an empty parking spot right by the front door.

"The sign," I said, pointing directly in front of us. It said "Reserved for Customers with Small Children."

"That is one prejudicial sign, don't you think? Small children should never be denied the opportunity to get exercise. That might explain why there's such an obesity problem in this country."

He turned off the engine and climbed out. I hesitated.

"Are you waiting in the car or coming in with me?" he asked.

Quickly I clicked off my seatbelt and joined him.

"Don't worry about the sign," he said. "It's not like parking in a handicapped spot. We don't need a special tag, and there's no fine for parking in these ones. Besides, having you along is almost like having a small child."

This guy was hilarious, and somewhat insulting at the same time.

"In fact, I'd like you to consider yourself my adopted child," he added.

"I hope you don't expect me to call you Daddy."

"To tell you the truth, I'm sort of working on having nobody calling me Daddy for a very long time."

I took a sip from my latte. I usually took my coffee black with one sugar and I'd never had a latte before. It wasn't bad. Ethan had got us our drinks while I grabbed a table. He'd plopped it down and told me I had to learn to drink like I lived in a city and not the sticks.

"I'm curious," Ethan said. "What's her name?"

"Whose name?"

"The girl who broke your heart."

Where did he get that from? I was just thinking it was none of his business and I wasn't going to say anything when he spoke again.

"Don't deny it. It's so obvious. I can see it in your eyes."

I'd seen it in my own eyes when I looked in the bathroom mirror. I just didn't know anybody else could see it.

"Well?" he asked.

"Jennifer . . . Jenn."

"Ah, never trust a Jennifer. That should be printed on T-shirts, posters, and bumper stickers." Almost against my will, and to my own surprise, I chuckled. "How long were you with her and how recent was the breakup?"

"We dated for almost three years, and the breakup was three weeks ago."

"Three years? You dated somebody for three years? That's like doing a prison term."

"Or practically being married," I added.

"That's what I said . . . a prison term. No, wait . . . oh no—you thought you were going to marry her!" he exclaimed.

"I didn't say that."

"You didn't need to. It's written all over your face. Part of you, deep down, on some sick level, still thinks you might somehow end up marrying her."

I felt like telling him to shut up, to get up and walk away, but I knew he was just pointing out the painful truth.

"She dumped you so hard you must have fallen on your head and sustained brain damage."

I'd barely met this guy—how was he reading the emotions I was trying to hide?

"Did she tell you that she couldn't handle a long-distance relationship?" he asked.

"Were you there?"

"No, I'm just aware of human nature. You might say I'm a student of how people think and react. Did you see it coming, or were you completely blindsided?"

"Looking back, I should have seen it coming but I didn't. I just thought we could work it out somehow, keep it alive despite the distance."

"I should have figured you for a romantic."

"I'm not a romantic," I scoffed.

"Even worse than a romantic is a romantic who doesn't know he's one. Romantics are the ones who get hurt. It's just a matter of time. So, did she do it in person, in a text, or through friends?" he asked.

"All of the above. I heard some things through the grapevine, and then I got a text telling me 'we have to talk,' and then it was face to face."

"Some people think face to face is the best way. I disagree. I'd rather be shot by a sniper from a distance than stabbed in the gut. Up close and personal is more brutal because they're looking you in the eyes when they plunge the knife into your heart."

"It wasn't like that," I said.

"Did it feel like that?" he asked.

I shrugged. It *did* feel like that. It still did. "But I guess she was right."

"What are you talking about?" he demanded.

"You know, long-distance relationships don't work. She was right to end it."

"Absolutely not! Her breaking up with you was so wrong."

"You think it could have worked?" I asked.

"Of course not, don't be stupid. I just mean that *you* breaking up with *her* would have been right."

"What?"

"You should have broken up with her. It's much

better to be holding the handle of the knife than having the blade stuck into you. Haven't you heard that it's better to give than receive?"

"I don't think that's what that expression means."

"Wrong again. And whatever you do, stop defending her."

"I wasn't defending her," I protested.

"Yes you were. Didn't you just say, 'I guess she was right'. . . twice?"

"Yeah, but—"

"No *buts*, no *ifs*, no *maybes*. Has she already started dating somebody else?"

I felt the knife in my stomach twist a little bit more. Even though it had been just over three weeks, the hurt was still there. It made me feel weak, vulnerable, like I'd somehow deserved it. Ethan was right, I had been defending her in my mind, making it seem like it was somehow my fault, either because I moved or because somehow she was right to break up with me.

Ethan gave a dramatic sigh. "You know, you don't even have to answer that question about her starting to date because I can see the answer in your expression. Who is he? Who is she dating?"

"Elmer."

"Elmer . . . that's . . . well . . . a completely ridiculous name. Who names their kid Elmer except for Mr. and Mrs. Fudd?"

"He's named after his grandfather, but even Elmer thinks it's a pretty stupid name."

"If you know that, you obviously know him. And my guess is that in a place as small as Hicksville—"

"Woodstock."

"Like it makes a difference? I just assume he has to be somebody that you knew fairly well."

"He was a friend." I couldn't admit he was just about my best friend.

"Then he's a bigger jerk than she is. Friends don't do things like that."

He chuckled, and I wanted to ask him what was so funny.

"By the way, this Elmer guy, he didn't crash your pickup or steal your dog, did he?"

"What?" I asked.

"I'm just wondering if this is really your life or the lyrics of a bad country song, that's all."

I laughed. It felt good to laugh.

"Graham, as you tell me this sad story, I realize that you need more than just a friend. I am here to become your mentor, your spirit guide on a journey of self-discovery in search of happiness. Think of me as a very good-looking, tall, tailored Yoda."

"And that makes me Luke Skywalker?"

"Yes."

"I've always been more of a *Star Trek* guy."

"That's simply a sign of how much you need my help. I will teach you to use the force. But I must warn you, there is a dark side."

"And we should avoid the dark side," I said.

"Oh, no, that's the side you should *embrace*. All the fun begins when it starts to get dark. Now, let us begin our journey. By the way, you chose a great table . . . excellent sightlines."

"Sightlines?"

"I can see everything, and everybody."

I looked around. We were in the middle of the mall, facing a big American Apparel store. Our seats were in a raised area by the coffee bar, and, as Ethan pointed out, we could see in every direction. But I wasn't sure why that was so good.

It was a big mall—much bigger than anything where I came from. There were so many people, so much action and activity. I was still a little bit thrown by the number of people and cars that buzzed around me every day. Not that I'd admit any of that to Ethan.

"Do you know the very best way to get over a girl and a bad breakup?" Ethan asked.

"Time?"

"Who has time for time? No, the best cure for one girl is a better girl."

"That would be hard to find in this case."

Ethan rolled his eyes and pushed his hand through his hair. "Spoken like a true romantic . . . or should I say a true *idiot*. No offence."

"None taken."

"So just how hot was she?"

"Jennifer was—"

"First rule of getting over her: don't ever call her by her name again. Naming her gives her more power over you. From now on she is simply *the girl*. Understand?"

Strangely, I did. "She was at least a nine."

"Little-town Hicksville nine? Or a real, big-city, not-dating-your-cousin nine?" Ethan asked.

"What does that even mean?"

"Let me explain the Theory of Relativity to you."

"What does Einstein have to do with this?"

"Not his theory, I mean the really important one. *Ethan's* Theory of Relativity."

Ethan then went on to explain it, and it went something like this. My school had four hundred students, half of which were female. That was a small sample group, from which *the girl* seemed hottest, but there weren't that many to compare her to. In a larger sample—like my new school, or the girls in the mall—she would not necessarily be as hot because there would be more, many more potentially *fine* young ladies. He added in all sorts of details, comparing fast cars to racing cars, good amateur athletes to professional athletes, and penguins to ostriches. I didn't really get the bird comparison, but this guy could really talk, and the more he talked, the more I sort of understood what he meant.

When he'd laid it all out, Ethan smiled at me. "Can you see how this makes logical sense?"

"Theoretically, it makes perfect sense," I agreed.

"Let's look around the mall. Find me somebody who you think is *the girl's* equal."

"That might take some time."

"While time is not the answer, today I have time. You have time. Come on, let's look around."

He got up quickly and walked away. I grabbed my cup, took a final sip, and took off after him, tossing the remaining latte in the garbage bin.

"Where exactly are we going to?" I asked.

"Going *to* implies a destination, and I prefer to think of this as a journey, or perhaps a hunt. Are you doing what I asked, looking around for a girl who is the equivalent number?"

"Yeah, but, like I said, it's not going to be that easy."

"Keep looking. Literally hundreds and hundreds of girls pass through these doors every day. Do you have a type?"

"Type?"

"You know, a type of girl who turns your crank, who gets you going, who causes you to stop thinking and almost bump into walls."

"That's hard to say," I answered.

"No it isn't. Tell me what *the girl* looked like."

"Well, she's blond —"

"Stop referring to her in the present tense. She is history, the past, so speak about her only that way, okay?"

I nodded. "She *was* blond, blue eyes, tall, almost five-ten, a great smile, and just, well, she had it going on."

"So basically she looked like that," he said, pointing to one of two girls who'd just come out of a store. Her long blond hair fell over one shoulder and she was smiling as she said something to her friend, who was smaller with short dark hair. They were about our age, maybe a little bit older.

"Um . . . yeah, there is a similarity for sure," I admitted.

"And how do you rate her on that same one-to-ten scale?"

"I don't know, maybe an eight. It's hard to tell without getting closer," I said.

"Okay, let's go and get closer."

"What?"

"We're going to walk over and talk to them, unless you think it would be better to yell at them from here. Is that how it's done in Hicksville . . . you 'holler' at them like it's a pig-calling contest at the county fair?"

"Of course not."

"Good, because here that will only attract mall security. Come with me, and try to follow my lead."

He walked right up to them. I trailed behind feeling awkward and uncomfortable.

"Excuse me," Ethan called out, and they stopped and turned around. "Would you mind doing me— us—a favour?"

"Possibly," the blonde answered. She looked skeptical. She also looked incredibly pretty. Maybe closer to an eight and a half.

"We were just wondering if you could take a photograph of us for the folks back home."

"You want us to take your picture?"

"I know it sounds pathetic, but we tried to take a couple ourselves, and we just ended up looking like a couple of country bumpkins who don't even know how to take a selfie."

I noticed that his voice had changed. He sounded less slick and more "country." He was talking a little more slowly. Was that what I sounded like to him?

"So, could you do it?" he asked as he held his phone out to her.

"We could do that," the blonde offered, and she took his phone from him.

"Come on over here, Greg. Get in close."

I nearly looked over my shoulder to see if "Greg" was there, but then realized he was talking to me. I smiled. Two could play that game.

"Sure thing, *Elmer*."

I wasn't sure why I picked that name but somehow it just seemed right.

He didn't miss a beat. "That's me . . . Elmer . . . like Elmer Fudd. Please don't make fun of my name. I'm a little sensitive about it."

"We would never do that," the brunette said. She sounded so genuine, like she really meant what she was saying.

We posed with Ethan's arm around my shoulder and the blonde took a few pictures of us.

"Are these okay?" the blonde asked as she handed him back his phone.

He looked through them, slowly, deliberately. "Greg always takes a good picture, but me, I just don't ever look right. Look at the goofy expression I have in this one." He turned the phone around and offered them the chance to see the pictures.

"You look good," the brunette said.

"Thanks for lying to make me feel better."

"I wasn't lying, honestly, you look good in these pictures."

"Only in the pictures?" he asked.

She looked embarrassed.

"You said you two were from out of town. Where are you from?" the blonde asked, rescuing her friend.

"It's a little place hardly anybody who isn't from there even knows about," Ethan said. He turned to me. "Tell 'em, Greggie."

I tried to think quickly. I almost said Woodstock but then I made something up instead.

"Buck River," I said, resisting the urge to give Ethan a big smile. "It's not much, only about five hundred people."

"It's so small it's not even on the maps," Ethan added.

"It's so small you have to leave town to change your mind," I added.

Ethan looked amused. "It's so small that when you drive you don't have to signal turns because everybody knows where you're going."

This was one contest I knew I could win. I knew more small-town jokes than he'd ever know. "It's so small that drag racing involves lawn tractors."

"It's so small that you can't avoid dating your friends' ex-girlfriends," he said.

I was wrong. He won.

"It's about ten hours north of here by car. It's pretty exciting for us to be down here in the city. I hate to admit it, but it's a little scary," I said.

"Scary how?" the blonde asked.

"It's just so big, and everything moves so fast," I said.

Ethan gave me a satisfied little nod, like he was saying, "Well done." Really, that was how I'd been feeling, so it wasn't like I was making anything up.

"Do you two girls think you could do us one more favour?" Ethan said. "This is a little embarrass-ing . . . just say no if you want . . . I'll understand."

"Go ahead," the brunette said.

"Our buddies were joking with us that city girls wouldn't even have the time of day for a couple of hicks from the sticks like us, and I was just wondering if, well, we could have somebody take a picture of the four of us and we could tell everybody that we went out on a date with two *beautiful* city girls."

I watched their faces and saw their reaction to being called beautiful. They looked a little bit embarrassed and a whole lot pleased. Before they could answer, Ethan asked a passing woman to take the picture and handed her his phone.

Ethan positioned us, with me beside the blonde and him between her and the brunette.

"Would it be all right if we put our arms around the two of you, just to sell the story to our friends?"

By way of response, the brunette snuggled into him as he put his arm around her.

"Is that okay?" I asked the blond girl.

She smiled. "It would look silly if only one of you was doing it."

Carefully, I put my arm around her—it felt strange to get so close to a complete stranger—and inhaled the flowery scent of her perfume. It smelled good. She smelled good. Almost overwhelmingly good.

The woman took a half dozen pictures, and handed the phone back to Ethan.

"I was just wondering, do we have to make up names to go with our made-up girlfriends, or can we use your real names?" Ethan asked.

"I'm Sierra," the brunette said.

"And I'm Jennifer," the blonde said.

Ethan looked at me and smirked. "That's amazing! Jennifer is Greg's *favourite* name in the world!"

"It is?" she exclaimed.

"Yes, it is."

They all continued to look at me, as if I should explain. I figured saying it was my old girlfriend's name—the girl who dumped me to date my best friend—was probably not the best way to go.

"It's my mother's name and my grandmother's name," I said, trying not to stumble over the lies.

"He also told me that someday he hopes it can be his daughter's name," Ethan said.

Both girls gave a little "aaah!"

"Me and Greg, we really don't know anybody in the city, and I was wondering . . . heck, I know it's stupid even to ask . . . a couple of girls as beautiful as you two, there's no way in the world that you wouldn't already be doing something on a Friday night."

The two girls looked at each other, nodded a little, and then turned back to us.

"We'd love to go out with you!" Sierra exclaimed.

"That's wonderful! Just wonderful!" Ethan said. "Now we can actually send those pictures and we won't be lying . . . I was never really comfortable doing that."

"Me neither," I said. No lying necessary for me there. "We really don't know the city very well. What do you think we should do?" I asked.

"We could go downtown," Jennifer said.

"Or we could just go to a movie here in the mall and maybe back to my place later," Sierra added.

"That would probably be better," Ethan said. "This is already way busier than we're used to, so downtown might be too much."

They both chuckled.

"Will your parents be all right with us coming over?" Ethan asked.

"I don't see why they wouldn't be . . . they're not going to be home until late tonight."

"If you give me an address, then we'll pick you two up at seven. Would that work?" Ethan asked.

"That would be wonderful," Sierra said.

"Great, give us your numbers and we'll see you at seven."

After we took down their numbers, Ethan reached over, put his arm around Sierra, pulled her close, and kissed her! I thought she might pull away but she didn't. She leaned into the kiss.

"There we are, sealed with a kiss," Ethan said to her.

I looked over at Jennifer, hesitating. Was I supposed to . . .? She held out her hand and we shook, and I felt relieved.

CHAPTER THREE

"Good morning, sugar plum."

I startled and sat up. Ethan was sitting on the edge of my bedroom dresser. I rubbed my eyes. "What are you doing here?"

"I just wanted to watch you sleep."

"Um . . . I . . . what?"

"Wait, that does sound really creepy. Actually, I just got here."

"What time is it?" I asked.

"It's almost ten. By the way, I didn't sneak in through your bedroom window. Your mother let me in. Your parents are very nice, and your sister is a real sweetheart. They insisted that I have a coffee with them before they sent me to wake you up. Now we can all have breakfast together. Oh, and just so you know, your parents—especially your father—they feel really guilty about you having to leave your old school and all your friends. You should use that guilt. It could be good for something."

"What sort of something do you mean?"

"Maybe you can use it to get a later curfew."

"I don't have a curfew."

"Okay, then a bigger allowance, or using the car more—although I've seen what's parked in your driveway, and I'd try to avoid ever driving around the city in that minivan."

It certainly didn't compare to his BMW.

"So, Foxy, you impressed me last night."

"Probably not as much as you impressed Sierra," I said.

"That's not so much a testament to how awesome I am as to how desperate she is. Thank goodness I love the smell of desperation." He jumped down from the dresser and moved over to my desk, looking over my books and papers. "What did you think of Jennifer?" he asked, still examining my stuff.

"I thought we weren't saying that name any more."

"We're not mentioning the name of one female. That doesn't mean we can't use the name for the other Jennifers who dot the landscape. So, what's the verdict?"

"I liked her. She was nice, pretty, a great kisser."

"*A great kisser,*" he said, shaking his head. "You saying that is so, well, so sweet and pathetic all at the same time."

"Pathetic? So now I'm pathetic."

"Not just now. And here's what's better than you liking her—I believe she likes you even more."

"Why is that better?" I asked, hoping he was right.

"You really are new to this relationship stuff, aren't you? Her liking you more than you like her gives you the hammer in the relationship."

"The hammer?"

"Every relationship has a hammer and a nail. Somebody has to have the edge, the control. Every relationship has somebody up and somebody down. The person who is up has the advantage, the hammer. In this relationship, right now, that's you."

"And if I don't want to have the hammer?"

"Then you're the nail. Would you like to see her again?" Ethan asked.

"Oh, definitely!"

"And so you shall. We'll call in a couple of days and arrange to see them . . . maybe two or three weeks from now."

"Why not sooner?" I asked.

"Don't you listen to anything I say?"

"I'm trying to avoid listening to everything you say. You talk a lot."

"I'll ignore that obvious cheap shot. It's about the hammer. Try to follow along. If you call right away, then you're giving her the hammer."

"So I'd become the nail?"

"Exactly! You were paying attention! You have to keep her waiting. If you call now, you'll be a nail that's already hammered down."

"How do you figure that?"

"If you call and ask her out, that will mean that you cancelled going home to Butt Kiss Lake so that you can see her. Doesn't that make you sound desperate?"

"Or sweet."

"No, desperate. Incredibly desperate. How are you going to explain to them why you're here and not on the road back to Butt Kiss Lake?"

"First off, it's Buck Lake." I paused. "And second, you're right. Why did we do that, anyway, tell them that we were leaving?"

"Two reasons. One, so we don't have to see them right now, and two, when we do see them again they'll think that we drove ten hours. Talk about earning bonus points. Does that make sense?"

"But doesn't driving all that way take away from me having the hammer?" I asked.

"You are thinking this through, and I'm impressed. Even though you're wrong. Driving down is sweet, and she will be impressed," he explained. "And when we do see them we'll go and see another romantic comedy, hopefully one that's not as pathetic as last night's."

"It wasn't that bad. I liked it."

He shook his head. "Are you actually a girl? Romantic comedies are chick flicks. No, wait, I forgot, you're a romantic, which makes you almost a chick. Gosh, you must have been so *pleased* and *surprised* at the end of the movie when the girl and the guy got back together. Wasn't that cute?"

"I totally saw that coming," I said.

"If you hadn't, I'd be even more worried. And it was so long! We should have been back at Sierra's place much earlier." He picked up one of my model planes from a shelf. "And speaking of cute . . ." he said.

I felt embarrassed. "I built them when I was little."

"And as soon as you moved here you put them back up on display. Maybe 'cute' was the wrong word. Let's go back to 'pathetic' again. But all these models actually explain a lot."

"What do you mean?"

"You've obviously smelled a lot of glue in your time."

"Nice, very nice," I said.

"Speaking of smell . . . I can smell the bacon. We're expected for breakfast. Your parents seem to like me. I can probably convince them to feed you as well."

"Gee, thanks."

"No thanks necessary. You know, you and I make a pretty good team, don't you think?"

"Yeah, it all worked last night. It worked really well."

"Graham, my friend, we are both, shall we say, free agents. You are new and—aside from me—friendless. Me, I've had my best buddies, my team, and my time stolen from me. But together we can have some real kicks. What do you say to a partnership that involves fun, females, frivolity, and a little bit of freaky?"

I thought about it. And I thought about how I needed a little bit of fun, and how I needed a friend.

"You've got yourself a partner."

"Good! Now let's get some breakfast."

He left the room, so I climbed out of bed, took a quick look in the mirror, ran my fingers through my

hair, and went to join him, making a quick detour to
the bathroom first.

Before I'd even reached the kitchen I could hear
laughter. He was entertaining them. Why wasn't I
surprised?

"Good morning, sleepyhead," my mother said.
She came and gave me a little kiss on the cheek.

"Late night," my father said.

"It was a great night!" Ethan exclaimed. "I guess
you didn't have time to tell your parents about your
date."

"Um . . . no."

He turned to my mother. "Are you interested in
hearing about it?"

"Sure. It would be a first, but that would be, well,
interesting."

I wasn't sure where to start or what to say or what
I shouldn't say. I was pretty sure I wasn't going to
mention the way we met them.

"Let's start with the basics," Ethan said. "Her name
is Jennifer. Yeah, we know, but this is a *better* Jennifer."

My sister Olivia practically did a spit take with
her orange juice, and my mother giggled.

"Think of her as sort of Jennifer 2.0. She's rede-
signed, with none of the annoying features that you
all came to dislike in the original," he continued.

"My parents didn't think she was annoying." I
looked up at them, and they both looked away. "You
didn't like her?"

"We liked her . . . most of the time," my mother
said.

"Well, she was a little bossy," my father admitted.

"A little?" Olivia said. "She was just about the most bossy person I'd ever met."

"Look who's talking?" I questioned.

"Come on, no fighting," Ethan said. "Tell them more about the date."

"There's not much to say. We met a couple of girls, Sierra and Jennifer, and we took them to a movie."

What I didn't say was that after the movie we'd gone back to their place and hung out, goofed around a little, and even had a couple of beers that Sierra had liberated from her parents. Then we left just before her parents were scheduled to come home, around 2:30.

"And it's nice that Jennifer 2.0 likes your son," Ethan said.

"You must be joking," Olivia said.

"No," Ethan said. "I'm pretty good at this stuff. Do you want me to list the ways she made it obvious?"

"How about if we pass on that," I suggested.

My father brought over the skillet. It was filled with bacon. I loved bacon. He forked out half a dozen pieces to each of us. The scrambled eggs were already in a big bowl on the table and we all helped ourselves.

"Thank you so much," Ethan said. "This is so kind of you."

Olivia jumped in before my parents could reply. "We should be thanking you for hanging out with my brother." I shot her an evil look.

"Well, I'm thankful that you're here with us for breakfast, Ethan. It's always good to get to know our children's friends," my mother said.

"You must have been worried about how hard this move was going to be on your kids," Ethan said.

Both my parents looked a little guilty—just the way he'd described it.

"I know it must have been hard, knowing that they were leaving behind all their friends, their schools, and all of that," Ethan went on.

"It wasn't easy," my father admitted. There was that look of guilt again, even stronger.

"It was hard for *all* of you," Ethan said.

"We also lost our dog," Olivia added.

"That was six months before," I said. "Our dog Lola died."

"I'm sorry to hear that," Ethan said.

"But we're getting another one," Olivia said. "In the spring, right?"

"Yes, once we've settled in a little more," my father replied.

"I feel settled," Olivia said. "Graham has a new friend, and maybe even a girlfriend. Isn't that settled?"

"Well, I'll do my part to help Graham settle in," said Ethan. "I just want you to know that, starting today, he's taken care of."

"That's kind," my father said. "Now, how about if everybody gets down to the serious business of eating some more breakfast?"

CHAPTER FOUR

The band was louder than it was good, but it was Saturday night and nobody seemed to care. All around the edges of the floor the stand-up tables were occupied by guys and girls, laughing, holding non-alcoholic drinks, and talking loudly enough to be heard above the noise. I'd never been in an all-ages dance club before. Heck, I'd never been in a dance club of any kind before. Ethan explained that the big difference was that there was no alcohol, so anybody who was old enough to drink legally was probably somewhere else. That explained why it seemed like a high school dance, only louder and with more people.

The dance floor was crowded—almost exclusively with girls. Over the half hour that we'd been here Ethan had been coming and going on what he called "scouting missions." I didn't know why he had to go on any "mission" to find girls—the whole place was filled with them. Seriously, the view was impressive. Nothing in my old town could possibly have compared to this.

Ethan appeared again just as the band finished up a number. There was a loud cheer, lots of clapping, and then they announced they were taking a twenty-minute break.

"What do you think of this place?"

"It's like I died and went to heaven!"

"Yeah, I try to come here once a month or so."

"Why wouldn't you be here every night?" I asked.

"It doesn't work that way."

I was going to ask him what exactly that meant, but I was afraid he'd make some crack about me not knowing how things worked because I was from Hicksville.

"Can I ask you a question?" I said.

"How will you learn if you don't ask questions? Shoot."

"Yesterday, why did we use false names?"

"It's always playful to be somebody else. Didn't you enjoy playing the game?"

I shrugged. "I have to admit it was fun."

"So, how did you know to give me a false name starting with E?" he asked.

"I don't know what you mean. I just called you Elmer because you thought it was a stupid name."

"It *is* a stupid name. But I called you Greg because it starts with the same letter as Graham. It's the first rule for fake names. Start with the same letter so if you start to blow it you at least have the first sound right and you have a chance to correct it," he said. "You know, you're a very convincing liar. I was impressed."

"Um . . . thanks . . . I guess."

"There's one more reason that we need to play a game. I know that you need to be protected."

"Protected from what?"

"From Jennifer."

For a split second I thought he meant *my* Jenn, but then I realized he meant the Jennifer we'd met at the mall. "She didn't seem all that dangerous."

"Anything that can inflict pain and suffering is dangerous. The more beautiful and desirable the female, the greater the danger involved." He paused, and I could almost see the wheels turning inside his head. "Let's say you started to see her and you got serious too fast—which is the natural rebound tendency of the heart, especially for a romantic like you—and let's say she broke it off suddenly. What would that do to you?"

Just thinking about that made my heart ache. "That would hurt a lot. It would be hard . . . really hard," I finally said.

"Right. And you can't afford to have somebody else do that to you right now. You were wounded. You don't want that wound to be ripped open before it has a chance to heal. That could kill you. You need to heal, get stronger. And maybe next time you'll get to be the one who does the dumping."

"You want me to dump Jennifer?"

"No. Well, a breakup's going to happen one way or another. You have to realize that almost every relationship you're ever going to have will end, usually badly. Let's say you date a hundred different females."

"I can't see that happening," I said.

"Stay with me and I can practically *guarantee* it. So, out of those one hundred relationships, ninety-nine will fail and one will ultimately succeed. Well, at least temporarily."

"And what does that mean?"

"Don't people ever get divorced in Hicksville?"

"I wouldn't know because I'm from Woodstock, but yes, people in Woodstock do get divorced."

"About half of all the couples who get married end up divorced."

"That's still a fifty-fifty chance of long-term happiness."

"Of course it isn't. Even most of the couples who do stay married aren't happy. They've just given up instead of leaving. So, with those odds, you would have to be a fool to bet on any one of your relationships being *the one*. You have to go into every relationship with an understanding that it's 99 percent certain it's going to fail. Does that make logical sense?"

"In a twisted mathematical way," I admitted.

"How many girls have you been with?" Ethan asked.

"Isn't that a little personal?"

"I don't mean *with* with, I just mean dated, gone out with."

"Four," I said, lying, because it was only three.

"Four? I've had busier weekends. Matter of fact, if you'd said three, I've had busier *days*. So, last night Jennifer became your fifth."

"I counted her in already," I mumbled, feeling embarrassed.

"You, my friend, need my help even more than I imagined. In fact, last night was all about you. That was basically me throwing myself on another grenade."

"I wouldn't describe Sierra as a grenade, exactly."

"Perhaps not, but I definitely threw myself on her," he said.

"Oh, very funny," I said. "But if you didn't think she was good enough for you, why didn't we try to find somebody better?"

"Waiting for 'better' increases the risks. Last night was pretty much a sure thing. You succeeded, and now you have Jennifer 2.0 in your back pocket. You have to admit, it did ease the pain a bit, didn't it?"

"No argument."

"And that's both good and bad," Ethan said.

"How could that be bad?"

"If you start feeling too good too fast, then you'll forget. You should never forget that feeling in the pit of your stomach, that pain that was inflicted on you. You have to remember it well enough to never want it to happen again."

As usual, on some gut level I understood exactly what he meant. I never wanted to have that pain again. Never. Ever.

"So, back to the here and now. Do you see anybody you'd like to meet?" Ethan asked.

"I see hundreds."

"Yes, but think zebra."

"I was thinking girl."

"Girl, zebra, it's all the same," Ethan said.

"You must have an even stranger dating life than I imagined."

"Do you want to hear my theory on this or don't you?"

"Do you have a theory on everything?" I asked.

"Pretty much. If I don't have a theory, then I have a rule."

"Okay, so tell me how zebras are the same as girls."

"Of course. Zebras, as you probably know from *National Geographic* specials, travel in herds. Their markings blur together so that predators chasing them, mainly lions, have difficulty identifying any one individual animal. So here's the point. You need to stop looking at the herd of girls before us and focus on a specific prey."

"It makes it sound like we're hunting."

"We are. I want you to identify the two hottest-looking females you can see."

"Already done. Two at the table to the far right of the dance floor, one is in red and the other is in blue."

"Actually, I saw them almost right away when we walked in, but it's nice to know that you saw them too. You are a fine young Simba."

"So, do we go over and talk to them?" I asked.

"You may have noticed that a lot of guys have been trying that, strolling over, bringing them drinks, asking them to dance."

"I've noticed." I'd seen the first set go up and figured I'd missed my chance. Until I saw them walk away looking dejected. Then it happened a second, and a third time.

"And I imagine you've also noticed that they are still alone and have not danced with anybody except each other?"

"Okay, I get your point. They're not interested, so forget about them, we leave them alone."

"I didn't say that. Do you think they came here to listen to this crappy band?"

"So you *do* think they're in play, and we could pick them up?"

"Everybody is in play."

"I can't wait to hear the great line you're going to use."

"Do you really think I have that magic line, that Holy Grail, available to me?"

"I was sort of counting on it," I said.

"I appreciate the confidence but it's ill-placed. There are good lines and bad lines but no magic lines. Let's study them for a bit. We're not the only ones who think they're hot."

We watched as two more guys sidled up to the table and started a conversation with them.

"Okay, even though we can't hear them, let me provide the dialogue for this encounter," Ethan said. "*Do you girls want to dance, have a drink, get to know us, want us to join you at your table, or would you maybe consider sleeping with us?*"

I laughed. "I'm not sure they would have actually said that last bit."

"It's implied. And they reply: *No, go away, you trolls! The nerve of you two to think that you're good enough to even breathe the same air we breathe.*"

44

He'd hardly finished when the two guys turned and walked away. They looked as if somebody had neutered them.

"And that, my friend, is why those two young women are here," Ethan said.

"They're here tonight to turn guys down?"

"Exactly. They are getting some perverse pleasure, enjoying some personal power, from having guys wreck themselves like ships against the rocks. Even from this distance, can't you see that they seem even more satisfied with themselves right now?"

I looked. If there was a difference, I couldn't see it . . . wait . . . they were smiling. Had they actually enjoyed turning those guys down?

"So you're saying that if we go up to talk to them, we'll not only be shot down, but they'll enjoy doing it?"

"Precisely," he said.

"But you still think they're in play, that we should ask them?"

"Of course."

"So . . . you want to get turned down?" I asked.

"*We* won't get turned down," Ethan said. "We will succeed, because it's our *duty* to succeed. It's like we know about the rocks just below the surface and yet we stand idly by as more ships crash and more lives are lost."

"Isn't that a little dramatic?" I asked. "Nobody died here tonight."

"Dramatic? Didn't you feel like you wanted to die when you were dumped?" Ethan asked.

I did. "So we should warn people to stay away from them?"

"Nobody would listen," he said.

"Then what are you suggesting?"

"Since we can't stop the ships, we remove the rocks!" he yelled. He pounded his fist against the table with such force that my drink bounced into the air and people at surrounding tables, including the two girls, turned to look.

"Okay, now you're just scaring me."

"No need for fear. It's all taken care of. When the time is right, you just watch and play along. In fact, you can start now by observing them closely."

I looked over at the two girls just as two more guys approached them. I would have felt sorry for them if I hadn't felt slightly afraid. Both guys were big—very big—and one had a significantly large scorpion tattoo on the side of his neck. I was pretty sure they were old enough to have been drinking at a real dance club.

"This is about to get really interesting, really fast," Ethan said.

The two guys moved up to the table and sort of shoved themselves in, so the two girls were separated with the two guys in the middle.

"That was a good strategy separating them like that," Ethan said. He was clearly going to give me the play-by-play commentary. He really did see all of this as a game.

The girls looked a little shaken, slightly hunched over and trying to ease away from the guys. Who could blame them? The scorpion tattoo guy reached over and took one of the drinks on the table and drained the glass!

"Wow, I didn't see that coming," I said.

"Neither did the girls. I think it's time. Let's go."

Before I had a chance to answer, Ethan started off toward them. I hesitated for a split second and then quickly caught up to him.

"What are you doing?" I questioned.

"We're going to tell those guys to shove off."

"You're insane!" I snapped. "We're going to be killed."

"Have faith," he said. "Just follow my lead."

We walked up to the table. The guys looked even bigger up close.

"Hey, gentlemen, how are you doing?" Ethan asked.

"There's no gentlemen here," Scorpion snarled.

"Just us two and our women," the other guy said.

"Are you two with them?" Ethan asked the girls.

"No, they just barged over and—"

"And you two better beat it right now if you don't want any trouble." Scorpion poked a finger at us ominously. He took a step forward, and I backed up half a step, but Ethan stood his ground. He was either a lot braver than I thought he was or much stupider.

Ethan cocked a finger and Scorpion came right up to him, until they were nose to nose, and I braced myself. Ethan was saying something to him but he was saying it so quietly that I couldn't hear it over the music.

I felt a powerful urge to turn and run, but I couldn't do that. No matter what, Ethan was my friend and I couldn't just abandon him. Alone, he'd get killed. Who was I kidding—*together* we were still going to get killed. I just hoped we'd get a few shots in before they pounded us silly. But then Scorpion just backed off!

Wide-eyed, I watched as he grabbed his friend by the arm and the two of them stumbled away, pushing people out of their way as they disappeared into the crowd and the darkness away from the dance floor.

Ethan turned to me, winked, and then looked over at the girls.

"Are you two all right?" he asked.

"We are now," the girl in the red dress said.

"But that was scary; they were really scary," the one in the blue dress added. "He looked like one of those guys from *America's Most Wanted*."

"Yeah, we saw them come up and we thought we'd better keep an eye on what was happening," Ethan said. "And when they didn't leave right away we knew there might be trouble and we'd better get over here."

"We really want to thank you!" Blue Dress said, and Red Dress nodded vigorously in agreement.

"That's nice, but no need to thank us. We just did what needed to be done. The important thing is that they took off. And we should probably do the same. It's obvious that you two just want to spend time together, so we'll leave you alone."

He turned to leave.

"Wait!" one of them yelled out.

He turned back around.

"Could we at least buy you two a drink . . . you know . . . a Coke, to thank you?" Red Dress asked.

"Well, it's certainly not necessary, we were just doing the right thing. But, come to think of it, it might be a good idea for us to stick around a little bit." He paused. "They could still come back. They didn't look like the kind of guys who take no for an answer."

The two girls suddenly looked more worried. I felt the same way. We all looked in the direction they had disappeared, hoping they weren't going to suddenly reappear.

"Do you really think they'll come back?" Blue Dress asked.

"It's hard to predict people like that. Somebody who gets a tattoo on his neck might have some impulse control issues going on," Ethan said.

"But I doubt they will, as long as we're here," I added. Was I trying to convince them or myself?

"Then you're definitely staying!" Red Dress grabbed my arm and pulled me in beside her.

Ethan made the introductions. This time I was some guy named Gilbert—Gillie to my friends—and he was Elliott. They were Tara and Christine— assuming they were giving us their real names.

"I'm curious, what exactly did you say to that guy?" Tara, a.k.a. Red Dress, asked.

I was pretty curious about that myself.

"It's not something I would ever repeat in front of ladies. It was rather crude," Ethan said.

"Weren't you afraid of what he might do?" Christine asked.

"People like that are usually just bullies. You call their bluff and they fold. Besides, I have a secret weapon." He turned to me. "Gillie here is a fourth dan black belt in karate."

"Wow!" Tara said.

"Behind those gentle good looks is the heart of a tiger, and fists of stone," Ethan said.

"Oh, look, you embarrassed him," Tara cooed.

I was blushing, but it was because the lie really threw me.

"Go on, show them a karate pose," Ethan said.

I was too stunned and confused to do anything.

"He's so modest," Ethan added. "If I had his skills, I think I'd be wearing my karate outfit all the time. What do you call those pyjama-looking outfits?"

"A karate uniform is called a *gi* and the belt is an *obi*," I said. My turn to throw him. "And that's what I'd call it if I had a fourth dan black belt in karate, but I don't."

The girls looked confused, and Ethan looked surprised . . . no, disappointed . . . no, annoyed!

"I've never taken karate," I said.

Now he looked completely pissed off. I had to admit, I was kind of enjoying being the one to surprise him, but now was the time to come clean. "You have to excuse my friend because he calls all martial arts 'karate.' I am into the discipline of Tae Kwon Do, which is also known as 'Korean karate.'"

"Oh," Christine said. "It's different."

"My uniform is known as a *dobok*," I explained.

Ethan looked not only relieved but amused. Hey,

he wasn't the only one who could play. And if those guys did come back, at least I'd be beaten up with a smile on my face.

"Gillie doesn't like people to know about any of this because he thinks it's bragging," Ethan said. "He hardly even talks to me about it. Sorry to blow your cover, buddy, but I figured it would make the girls feel safer and more comfortable."

"It does make me feel better," Tara said. She edged closer to me.

"I almost hate to admit how skilled he really is. If I hadn't told you, you'd probably still think I was being really brave coming over to rescue you, but that would have been dishonest," Ethan said. "And I'd just feel guilty if I wasn't telling the truth."

Now that was a double, or maybe a triple lie. I couldn't figure it out.

"I knew that I could have just stepped back and Gillie would have handled those two guys all by himself." He stopped, and it looked as though he was thinking. "Of course, it would have been a lot risker if there had been four or five of them . . . wait . . . do any of you wonder if they only went away to get some backup?"

Judging from their expressions and the knot that instantly formed in my stomach, nobody but Ethan had thought of that.

"Look, there's nothing to worry about, they're probably not coming back at all, but still . . . I think it might be better if you two relocated," Ethan said.

"To a different table?" Christine asked.

"I think it would be better to go to a different place. It might be wise if you left. Do you two have a ride?"

"We were going to cab it," Tara said.

"We can wait with you outside and put you safely in a cab, or we can drive you. Whatever you want we'll do," Ethan said. "We're just here to make sure you're safe. Guys like those two, when they get angry, well . . . if they can't take it out on us, they might try to take it out on you."

The two girls looked at each other like they were trying to telepathically decide. I just wanted them to decide quickly before those guys—and maybe some of their friends—reappeared and my almost nonexistent martial arts training was put to the test.

"Here's the problem with a cab, though. What if they're waiting outside in the shadows somewhere, and they see you get in the taxi and decide to follow you?" Ethan said.

Their uncomfortable look slipped into one of fear.

"And we wouldn't be waiting at the other end to protect you," Ethan continued.

"If you could drive us, that would be great," Tara said.

"We'd be more than happy to do that," Ethan said, reassuringly.

"Thank you so much!" Christine exclaimed. "But could I use the facilities before we leave?"

"Yeah, I need to pee too," Tara said.

"No problem," Ethan said.

Great, more delay. "But it might be a good idea to hurry," I suggested.

"Yeah, we wouldn't want Gillie to have to hurt somebody if they come back," Ethan said.

We walked away from the table by the brightly lit dance floor, and I felt better as we moved into the dimmer part of the club close to the washrooms.

"We'll wait right here," Ethan said. "Don't worry, you're safe in there . . . but please hurry."

They rushed off, disappearing into the washroom.

"Do you really have training in Tae Kwon Do?" Ethan asked.

"Oh, sure, extensive. I took about a dozen classes when I was ten. I still have the outfit in my closet. Do you want to see it?"

"Maybe later. You had me going for a bit there. Impressive. Just out of curiosity, do you still have any martial art moves?"

"Oh, yeah, I could strike a pose that might make people think I know what I'm doing."

"Enough to scare somebody?" he asked.

"If they aren't very bright. If you keep doing things like you did here, I have a feeling that I might need to actually try to defend us. That was crazy."

"Crazy like a fox . . . well, not a Graham Fox, but a really clever fox."

"Getting us killed isn't clever. All I want to do is get out of here so we're safe," I said.

"We're completely safe. No need to worry about anything," Ethan said. "Bruno and his brother weren't actually going to hit us."

"Bruno? Who's Bruno?"

"The big guy with the scorpion is Bruno."

"Wait, when did he tell you his name?"

"Two or three years ago. I guess we've been friends for about that long."

I was stunned. "You mean that . . . that . . . the whole thing was just a . . . a . . .?"

"A scam, part of the game. I met the guys on one of my trips around the club—I said hello and bought them a Coke. I asked them to do me a favour and they agreed it would be fun. Now that you know what was going on, you have to admit, it's pretty hilarious."

"Yeah, I always think being terrified of getting the crap kicked out of me is a real laugh-fest. Why didn't you tell me what you were going to do?"

He shrugged. "I wasn't sure if you could pull it off, so I thought I'd use your natural reactions as a way to sell it, and it worked." He paused. "It was almost more fun that way. You should have seen your face a couple of times."

"You are such a jerk," I said.

"You're calling the guy who scored you one of the two hottest women in the place a jerk? I think the word you're looking for is 'genius.' I knew I needed to change the dynamics and I believe it worked. Wouldn't you agree?"

"I agree that we're driving two girls home."

"Not necessarily home. These two are done like dinner. When we get to the car you make sure you climb into the back seat. That way they can decide who's going to be with which of us. I think Tara's going into the back seat. Would you like to make a bet?"

"I don't think I ever want to bet against you."

ERIC   WALTERS

"Smart man."

Before I could say anything else they emerged from the washroom, flashing us big smiles.

Tara came over and took my arm. No need to wait until we got to the car. Ethan was right again. They'd probably been having a discussion in the washroom about who was going to be with who.

"I feel so much safer knowing that you're here. Thank you." She snuggled into me as we started to walk. I could feel the eyes of other people on us as we walked out—the two most beautiful girls in the place were leaving with us.

Okay, Ethan had been a jerk not telling me about what he was doing, but he also *was* a genius. An evil genius, but a genius nevertheless.

CHAPTER FIVE

"Wake up, sunshine."

My eyes popped open, worked hard to focus, and then I saw Ethan leaning overtop of me. Did he sneak into my bedroom again? What was wrong with this guy? Then I realized I wasn't in my room. I was in the back seat of Ethan's car, with the top still down, in one of the parking lots outside the college dorm. The stars had been replaced by a rising sun.

"I fell asleep," I mumbled, sitting up and rubbing my eyes.

"You passed out."

"I didn't have that much to drink."

"Then I guess it was your identical twin who was throwing back all that beer."

"It must have been. I hate beer."

"Then you were doing a wonderful job of faking it."

I started thinking back, and I remembered beer, more than a few beers, going down. There was a horrible taste in my mouth, and even more horrible thoughts in my head as the evening started to become real again.

"Come on up front. We should get going."

I climbed over the seat just as he started the engine. We drove off without wasting any more time.

We'd driven the girls back to their sorority house. They were in their freshman year at college and had come to the club because they actually did like that terrible band. At their suggestion, when we drove them back to campus we all went to a big kegger at a frat house down the way. That was when things got both dicey and blurry.

"You'd really think a university student like yourself would be able to handle his alcohol better," Ethan said.

That was a part of our thread of lies for the night. It was something that Ethan called "mirroring." Yet another of his theories. When we found out they were in first year college, then so were we. When we found out their favourite music, then that was our favourite music. We even claimed that we liked that terrible band. Ethan talked about how doing this built "commonality and comfort," and from the little I'd seen it worked awfully well. The hard part was remembering all the things I'd claimed to be. The hardest part was saying that their crappy musical tastes were also mine. How could any winner of a TV singing contest ever be your favourite singer?

"You have Tara's cell number, right?" Ethan asked.

That much I remembered. I pulled a slip of paper from my shirt pocket.

"Can I have it?" he asked.

I handed it to him. He held his hand high in the air and released it, and the breeze grabbed it and whisked it out of sight!

"What are you doing?" I yelled.

"I'm saving you from being hurt again. That girl was going to be nothing but trouble. Both of them. I already tossed what's her name's number."

"Christine. Her name was Christine."

"Whatever. History is called history because it's in the past and over."

"But they were both amazing . . . you know, beautiful and nice."

"They were spectacularly beautiful, and spectacularly *not* nice, and spectacularly dangerous. You may have been too inebriated to notice but that fight you almost got into was because of Tara."

More memories. One of Tara's old boyfriends had been there, and she'd sort of ragged on the guy until he finally said something back, and that almost caused me to get into a fight with him . . . and two of his friends.

"It was also just a matter of time—a very short time—before she would have handed you your walking papers. Do you think she'd really be interested in some high school guy?"

"She thinks I'm in college too."

"In a college that's a hundred miles away. Besides, she's not looking for some lowly first-year student. She's after somebody older and definitely richer."

"You can't know that."

"Yes I can. That sorority is full of rich girls. Didn't you see the jewellery she was wearing? That pendant around her neck was worth half as much as this car."

"Really?"

"I can *smell* money—I'm used to that smell. And it generally comes with an attitude. Look, don't get caught up in some fantasy about what could have been, because it couldn't. Enjoy what you had—a fantastic night at a frat party, drunk, with the hottest girl you've ever been with in your entire life. If, at the start of last night, I'd promised you that, you would have been ecstatic. Right?"

I laughed. "You're right."

He reached out and offered me his hand for a high-five.

"By the way, after you passed out, I took your phone and sent a text to your parents," Ethan said.

"You did what?" I demanded.

"I had to let them know that you were sleeping at my place so they wouldn't be worried when you didn't come home."

In the rush of everything I'd forgotten all about that! Or maybe I could blame that on all the beer.

"Your mother texted back, said she loved you and hoped you would . . . I believe it said 'sleep tight, and don't let the bedbugs bite.' You can check it on your phone if you want. I texted back your love as well and that you'd be home just after breakfast. Are you hungry?"

"My stomach's a little sensitive but some food might settle it down."

"I know the perfect place to grab breakfast. Wide selection and the food is free."

Ten minutes later I found myself in front of a huge house. I had figured from Ethan's fancy car that his family had money, but until then I'd had no idea how much. I got out of the car and found myself gawking at the huge stone-and-glass mansion in front of me. My family's house was nice, but this was another ten rungs up that ladder.

We went in through the front doors and along an elegant hallway lined with paintings. In the kitchen, I gazed around at all the marble and granite and the professional grade appliances. It was almost bigger than the entire main floor of my house.

Ethan introduced me to their cook, Berta, who offered to make us anything we wanted. My stomach growled as I sat chatting with Ethan and watching Berta work. This wasn't exactly my father standing at the stove and offering some bacon and eggs.

"Thank you," I said as she placed the plate in front of me.

"You are very welcome," she said with a hint of a Spanish accent. She had happy eyes that sort of twinkled when she smiled.

"You're the best, Berta!" Ethan said as she put a plate in front of him. "Thanks for getting up to make us breakfast."

"I was getting up anyway. Besides, you couldn't make yourself dry cereal."

"I could if you'd just give me the recipe."

She laughed and then reached out and gave his cheek a little squeeze. "You are lucky you are very cute." She paused. "Maybe too cute for your own good. Call if you need more."

I dug into my pancakes. She had made them to order with strawberries and blueberries, and they were really, really good. She'd also made a ton of bacon, some sausages, and there were homemade muffins.

"I can't believe you have a cook."

"If we didn't have Berta, we'd probably starve to death," he said.

"Your mother doesn't cook?"

"How incredibly sexist of you to assign that role to my mother and not my father."

"I didn't mean to—"

Ethan laughed. "You are *so* easy. My father cooks less than me. My mother does cook, it's just that she does her cooking halfway across the country."

"I didn't know that your parents were divorced. Sorry."

"Nothing for you to be sorry for, unless you were the one sleeping with my mother," he said. I was too stunned to say anything—and then I saw him smile. "Not that I blame her," he continued. "My father was no better behaved. Believe me, it's much nicer around here now. I can testify that a happy divorce is much better than an unhappy marriage."

"I guess so," I said, thinking this helped to explain his attitude toward long-term relationships.

"You might meet my father, but I'm not sure he's even home. He's been making up for lost time himself since he and my mother split."

"It's just you and your father?" I asked.

"Older brother as well—Todd—but he's away at law school. Very bright, great potential, pride of the family, chip off the old block, potential flag-bearer of the clan and my father's law firm."

"So what kind of lawyer is your dad?"

"Corporate law. Crime apparently doesn't pay but corporate does, especially if you're the lawyer."

"This is a very big house for just the two of you."

"Three, if you count Berta."

"I mean family."

"I see Berta a lot more than I see my father." He gulped down the rest of his orange juice, then banged the glass down on the counter. "Enough of this stuff; it sounds rather pathetic. Poor little rich boy living a lonely life in an empty mansion."

"To afford all of this, your father must be a very good lawyer."

"I don't know if he's good or just successful. With lawyers that can be two very different things. What did Shakespeare say about lawyers?"

"'The first thing we do, let's kill all the lawyers,'" I said. "It's from *Henry VI, Part 2*." I loved Shakespeare. My old grade ten English teacher, Ms. Greene, had said—and it stuck in my head—that Shakespeare had written every storyline that could be written, and everything since then had just been a variation on those themes.

"Impressive. My mother would certainly agree with that, starting with my father and then moving on to his divorce lawyer. I'm not sure why anybody would even want to be a lawyer . . . wait . . . there's a lot of money in it." He gestured around the kitchen. "He's very good at convincing people to believe whatever he wants them to believe."

"Sounds like his son."

"In some ways I guess I *am* a chip off the old block."

"All this stuff about girls, about people, how do you know all these things you've been showing me?"

"A lot of it is simply trial and error. They say practice makes perfect, and I've practised. But I've also studied it. I read books about human behaviour, social psychology, behaviour modification. Plus, I pick things up from my shrink."

"You see a psychiatrist?"

"Don't sound so surprised. If you'd come through the craziness that was this home you might want to talk to somebody too. According to my psychiatrist, I have some issues around anger, and suppression and redirection of emotions," Ethan said. "Do you know what that means?"

"Not really?"

"It means my psychiatrist can continue to suck money out of my father for years to come. That's a big part of why I see him."

"So you see a psychiatrist out of spite?"

"It's not the primary reason, but it's certainly a big secondary benefit. Look, if nothing else, I've come to realize that we're all screwed up in one way or another. That's simply what makes us who we are. You, however, probably don't think you're screwed up at all, do you?"

"I'd like to think I'm normal."

"Denial. I've been told that we're all locked into denial . . . of course, I deny that completely. So, what about your family?" he asked.

"There's not much to tell. It's my parents, you've met them, me, and my sister."

"Original mother and father, not steps, right?"

"Original mother and father. They've been married for twenty-three years."

"Happily?"

"Very happily. You probably saw that at breakfast."

"Anybody can fake anything for an hour or so. My parents were charming when they were out in public together."

"Maybe you should come over for dinner, spend more time at our place."

"Generally a cup of coffee is as much time as I want to spend around anybody's parents, but I might take you up on that. It would be like an anthropological study. I could take notes, maybe film a little and add narrative afterwards, and make it into a documentary." He put on a snooty British accent. *"Here we have the very elusive and rare happy marriage. Recently placed on the endangered list, many believe that it will ultimately exist only in isolated pockets or perhaps in game preserves."*

I couldn't help but laugh.

"Just out of curiosity, your parents didn't happen to be high school sweethearts, did they?"

I felt the urge to lie but I didn't. "They started dating in their high school sophomore year."

"Like you and the girl we cannot name."

"We started dating a year earlier."

"This explains a lot. A whole lot," Ethan said.

I guess it did.

Just like the stuff he'd told me explained a lot about him, too. There were a whole lot of complicated layers going on there inside his head, and I realized I was just starting to scratch the surface.

CHAPTER SIX

It was hard getting up early to go back to school on Monday. I spent a lot of time doing homework on Sunday, but as I sat down to dinner that night, I realized I hadn't thought of Woodstock, or anybody there, all weekend. And I figured things at school would be looking up too, now that I was friends with Ethan.

I balanced my tray in one hand and my books in the other as I wove my way through the cafeteria. Ethan had invited me to have lunch with him and a bunch of his friends—who, hopefully, would soon become my friends. I knew he would have liked to eat with his basketball buddies but that couldn't happen. These were his second-choice friends. I had to wonder if that was me, too—was I a second choice, after Glenn? He'd told me that Glenn had often gone out with him on these adventures.

Ethan seemed to attract people to him. "Frosty" was pretty popular, and that was good for me. It wasn't like being with my old friends—kids I'd started kindergarten with—but it was a whole lot better than being alone. And probably better than being around my old friends just then.

I couldn't help wondering how Elmer and Jennifer were doing, and I felt a stab of jealousy that surprised me a little. Were they sitting at "our" table in the cafeteria? I forced the image of them together out of my mind. I was here now, they were there, and it was all in the past.

Then I thought about something my history teacher had said in class that morning: "Those who cannot remember the past are condemned to repeat it." I was never going to let that happen to me again. I wouldn't forget.

Ethan was always the centre of attention, and being beside him put me there as well. I wasn't sure if the attention was always positive, but it was better to be envied or hated than pitied. Frankly, I was happier being the friend of the cool jerk than being the guy who'd lost his girlfriend to his best friend. Ethan was a lot of things, and loyal was certainly one of them. He would never betray me. He was the guy who jumped on grenades for his friends.

Ethan and the guys were already at the table and they greeted me as I sat down. Ethan was holding court. He had more jokes and stories than anybody I'd ever met. Despite what he'd said about lawyers, he would have made a great one—that or a used car salesman, or even a politician—*especially* a politician.

"I was just telling the boys about the weekend we had," Ethan said.

Hopefully, the fact that I passed out in the back seat of his car wasn't one of the parts he was highlighting.

"College girls!" One of the guys—his name was Tim—hooted.

"I can't believe you got her to give you money," James said.

I looked at Ethan. What was this guy talking about?

"Not give. Loan. I told her I needed to fill my gas tank and I'd forgotten my wallet. I promised to pay her back the next time I saw her."

"But you're never going to see her again," I said.

"That's the beauty of it. It's not like I lied. If she can find me, I'll give her back the money she lent me."

"You gotta take me along with you some time!" Tim cried.

"Your time will come, Grasshopper," Ethan said. "Right now you are but a boy, and this is the work of men. Besides, I'm sticking with Graham here." He reached over and gave me a pat on the shoulder. "He's a natural, one of the best wingmen I've ever had."

"Better than Glenn?" somebody asked.

"Glenn left big shoes to fill—size fourteen, in fact—but Foxy here is a fast learner. He's not as good yet, but he's going to be better."

"We should get going," Tim said. "We have an AV Club meeting to get to." The three of them said their goodbyes, leaving us alone at the table.

"I can't believe the AV Club guys are my friends now," Ethan said when they were out of earshot. "How the mighty have fallen when an AV geek even suggests he should come out with me. By the way, I have something planned for Wednesday night. Are you in?"

"Sure . . . maybe . . . what do you have in mind?" I asked.

"Why the hesitation? Hasn't this worked out well so far?"

"Not bad. Still, what are you thinking?"

"If I told you, it wouldn't be a surprise."

I chuckled. "Okay, surprise me."

"One more thing I love about you is that—uh-oh, wait, this looks like trouble," he said.

I turned to look where he'd been looking. There was nothing but a girl—a very good-looking girl—walking toward us. She didn't look dangerous but she certainly didn't look happy. However, even the snarl didn't change the fact that she was hot.

Apparently, Ethan wasn't universally liked; he was also hated. Maybe it was only a few of the girls, but what they lacked in numbers they made up for in intensity. If looks could kill, I'd have been getting ready to be a pallbearer at his funeral.

"Hello, Helen, how are you?" Ethan asked, flashing her his best smile.

"Drop dead, you fake, stupid, lying jerk," she replied.

As she passed she reached out a hand and knocked over his drink. The two of us jumped up to avoid having the orange juice spill all over us.

"Nice to see you, too, Helen!" Ethan said, his voice still sweet, his tone even, as she walked away.

"What was that about?"

"I dated Helen a couple of times."

"I understand that breakups can be emotional," I said.

"Those two dates were *two years* ago. Apparently, elephants, and some girls, never forget. What's that expression? 'Hell hath no fury like a woman scorned'?"

"I've noticed that there are some other girls in the school who seem to . . . dislike you."

He laughed. "'Dislike' is putting it mildly. I would say that there are some who simply *loathe* me, who see me as the lowest form of life, who would cheer if I were hit by a truck."

"That sounds a little extreme."

"Do you think so? Helen once tried to run me over with her car."

"Now you're kidding."

"It was in the school parking lot. I don't think she would necessarily have hit me but she did come racing along, her horn blaring, and I jumped out of the way before I could find out. By comparison, knocking over my drink is both a step forward and a kind and gentle act on her part."

"You do have a way with the ladies."

"And that's why it's so much better that they don't know where you live or where you go to school, won't ever see you again, and don't even know your real name," he said.

"At the risk of being obvious, maybe you should try not making them so mad."

"It's not my fault if they cannot handle the consequences of living without me. Listen, when you and what's her name broke up—when she broke up with you—what was it like to see her around the school after that?"

"Not good."

Awful, terrible, painful, like a knife in my heart is what I wanted to say. It was two weeks between the breakup—her dumping me—and me leaving the school. Seeing her was unavoidable. We had two classes together, our lockers were almost side by side, and we had the same lunch period. In a small school, there was no place to hide, nowhere I could go without running into her.

"And then it must have felt even worse when she started dating somebody in your school, right?" Ethan asked.

"Yeah, that was even worse," I agreed. They'd be walking in the halls together, holding hands, laughing. And it always felt like they were laughing at me. As I thought about it now, I felt an ache in my chest.

"And he was, as I recall, your so-called friend," Ethan said.

"My friend from grade school."

"You know what I think about that? He was no friend. He was never your friend, or he wouldn't have done that. I can promise you that I would never, ever date somebody you had dated without your express written permission."

"You make it sound like a business deal."

"Taking care of your friends is important business. Would you have dated his ex-girlfriend?"

I shook my head.

"The guy was a bigger jerk than the girl. Wouldn't it have been easier if you hadn't had to see her, or even worse, the two of them together? There are so many fish in the sea, we don't have to dip in our lines here in this tiny pond. Even a rat is smart enough never to crap in its own hole," he said.

"Another theory?"

"You can call it a theory or a rule or simply a fact, as irrefutable as gravity."

"I guess I've never heard it put that elegantly, and I'm not arguing. You haven't been wrong so far."

"Although you're silently judging me for taking money from our dates, right?" he asked.

"I didn't say that."

"You didn't have to. I can read you like a book. You know I didn't do it for the money. I did it for mankind."

"Okay, you're going to need to explain that to me."

"Simple. Those two were pretty full of themselves. We saw only a small sample of the swath of rejection that they left in their wake that night at the club. By doing what we did, by taking her money, never calling them again, we served notice that they are not as special as they think they are. Maybe they'll think twice now about tromping on other people's hearts."

"Well," I said, "I'm pretty sure they'll at least think twice now about lending money to random guys."

"You must admit it's kind of a kick that she paid for the gas we're going to use to find the next two girls lucky enough to meet us. I should make a note about this."

He pulled out his phone, opened the Note app, and started tapping something in.

"Are you really taking notes?" I asked.

"I record every encounter. It's part of the historical record, and it allows me to review my techniques."

I shook my head. This was unbelievable and completely believable all at once.

"Are you planning on writing a book?" I asked.

"Great idea! The title could be something about the art of picking up girls."

I had to laugh. I could almost visualize the cover.

"But on second thought, I wouldn't do that. This information is too dangerous, too powerful. I can't let this wisdom fall into just anybody's hands. It's only for the trusted few. People like you."

"I guess I should be honoured."

"No guessing about it."

There was one thing I didn't need to guess about right then, and that was how lucky I was to have Ethan as a friend.

CHAPTER SEVEN

Two days later, I found myself walking beside Ethan into a grey-brick building, a community centre. It wasn't our community, though—this was in another part of the city altogether. That fit Ethan's pattern: too close to home wasn't too good.

The city was so big it was anonymous. There was almost no chance of running into somebody by chance a second time. Where I came from, none of what Ethan did would have worked because everybody knew everybody, or at least *knew of* everybody. What was the point of a fake name when everybody already knew who you were?

He led me up the stairs to the fourth floor.

"I have to admire you, Foxy, for not pestering me with questions about what tonight is going to be about."

"You're welcome. But I did look at the white-board in the lobby that lists the evening's activities. So, are we here to learn how to draw, quilt, cook, or throw a pot?"

"None of the above . . . although someone did throw a pot at me once."

"Another less than satisfied ex-girlfriend, I assume."

"Correct once again."

"So why are we here?" I asked.

"Patience, patience. This is going to be an incred-ible test of your ability to perform."

"Perform?"

"'All the world's a stage . . .'"

"'And all the men and women merely players,'" I said, completing the quote. I'd had a part in our school play, *As You Like It*, last year. Jennifer had been in it too—and remembering that gave my heart a sudden ache. When was this going to stop?

"You do know your Shakespeare. Impressive." He smiled. "But we'll soon see just how impressive you can be."

Suddenly I didn't feel very confident. What did he have in mind?

Ethan led us into a room at the end of the hall. I was relieved to see that it held a bunch of kids—almost all our age—and most of them were girls, milling around the room and getting refreshments from a table in the corner. We moved over, nodding and saying hello and helping ourselves to cookies and lemonade. They all seemed very friendly, but that still didn't answer the question—what was this group

THE ART OF PICKING UP GIRLS

about? I didn't see any pottery or art supplies or basically anything. It was just the refreshment table and a
bunch of grey metal chairs assembled in a big circle.

I took a bite out of one of the cookies. It was
store-bought and slightly stale. I had to assume the
cookies weren't the reason we were there.

"Can we take our seats, please?" a woman called out.

I turned around. She was the one person in the
room who was older. Quickly, people settled into
chairs, and Ethan deftly manoeuvred us so that we were
sitting between the two best-looking girls in the place.
I should have seen it coming. Did he ever not notice?

"I want to thank you for all coming out tonight,"
the woman said. "It's good to see old friends and new
faces. Now, who would like to start?"

A girl at the far end of the circle raised her hand
and then got to her feet.

"Hello. Most of you know me, but for those who
don't, my name is Grace."

"Hello, Grace!" they all called back.

"My mother has a problem with alcohol and it
has affected my life. I'm here tonight, again, to look
for support in helping me to understand the issues
and help me move forward in my life. Thank you."

Everybody clapped, and I clapped along. I looked
over at Ethan. He was clapping louder than everybody
else, and he gave me a sideways, smug smile. I'd seen
scenes like this on TV shows. These were people who
had problems with alcohol, or had family members
with problems. I was a little stunned. And more than a
little angry. We shouldn't have been there. This was

just, well, wrong. But what could I do? I couldn't very well get up and leave without making a stupid scene.

Person by person, they went around the circle reciting the problems that alcohol or drug use had caused their families. Sometimes they'd tell stories about drunken parents, police being called, furniture or windows being smashed, having to go to the police station with a grandparent to bail out a parent. With each story I became more uncomfortable. A couple of times I tried to catch Ethan's eye but he wasn't looking at me. Was that deliberate or just the way the seats were aimed?

"That leaves our two new faces," the leader said. "Would one of you like to share your story?"

Uncomfortable made a sudden leap into panic, but before I could think of anything to say, Ethan got to his feet.

"Hello, my name is Ellis."

"Hello, Ellis," they all answered back.

"When I walked in here tonight, my first meeting, I didn't think that I'd be able to share," he said. "But being in this room, hearing your stories, seeing all of you being so brave . . . you've given me the courage to go on. I want to thank you for that."

"That's why we're here," the woman said, and others nodded in approval or offered quiet words of agreement.

The girl beside him reached over and patted him on the back. "We're here for you."

"Thank you, thank you so much. You have no idea how much that means to me."

I had a sudden thought. Maybe we weren't here as part of some con to pick up girls. Maybe we were here because Ethan *needed* to be here. Was that the story behind his parents' divorce? Had he brought me with him to give him the strength to attend? Now I felt bad for thinking bad things about him making me come here.

"I'm here because alcohol destroyed my life." He turned to the girl who had patted him on the back. "It was your story in particular that moved me, because my mother, too, was seriously injured in a car crash due to her drinking."

Was he or was he not telling the truth? Had his mother been in a car accident and he hadn't mentioned it? Or was this just another story? Were we here for real reasons . . . was he using a fake name to remain anonymous? Or was this all a lie? I felt completely confused. And then, as he went on and on, I realized he was adding details that I knew had nothing at all to do with his life. This was just part of the game, and he was playing it very well.

The girl beside him looked like she was going to cry. Others oohed and aahed. And if I hadn't known better, I would have believed him myself. This was all just another performance, another stage, and I had a front-row seat. He finished, and there was a round of clapping, louder than for anybody else.

"That was very brave, very brave," the leader said. "That leaves just one more person. Do you want to share your story?" she asked me.

"My friend, Grant, is pretty shy," Ethan said. "This might be hard for him to do." He gave me a look—a smirk. "I can't imagine that Grant will want to talk tonight."

He was offering me both an escape and a very deliberate challenge. It crossed my mind that I should tell the truth, out us both as phonies. But I wasn't that brave. Still, I wasn't going to just sit there and let him think I couldn't handle this. I got to my feet.

"Hello, my name is Grant," I said, hesitating over the name he'd given me. They all said hello.

"In my family it's not alcohol, it's drugs. Lots and lots of drugs."

The girl to my right had talked about her father's drug use. If I was going to make up a story, it only made sense to mirror hers. It wasn't up to the standards of the story that Ethan had crafted—after all, he'd had time to think his through—but it was good enough to get a round of applause and encouragement for being "brave enough" to share.

"I'm proud of you, buddy," Ethan said as he reached out and shook my hand. Then, to my complete surprise, he threw his arms around me and gave me a big hug. "Just so proud!" He sounded as if he were on the verge of tears. He was good. Really, really good. I was impressed, but also more than a little unnerved.

"I think this is a good time to take a fifteen-minute break," our leader announced.

"How about we go to the washroom?" I said, with a hard look at Ethan.

"I don't need to go to the washroom." He turned back to the girl beside him, but I wasn't going to let him off that easy.

"Please," I said firmly, my hand on his arm, already guiding him out of his chair.

He smiled at the girl. "We are here to support each other, right?"

She flashed him a big smile back, and we headed out the door. I didn't say anything until we got into the men's room and I did a quick check of the stalls to make sure we were alone.

"We shouldn't be here."

"In the washroom?" He glanced at himself in the mirror with a little smirk.

I was suddenly even angrier. "You know what I mean. Is that why you didn't tell me where we were going?" I demanded.

"I didn't tell you because I wanted to surprise you."

"I was more than surprised. This is wrong."

"Wrong? It's actually a stroke of genius worthy of da Vinci."

"I don't think either Einstein or da Vinci ever faked an addiction problem in his family to pick up women," I said.

"Da Vinci was too busy wasting his time making flying machines and painting ceilings."

"Ceilings?"

"You know, the Sistine Chapel."

"First off, it was Michelangelo who painted the ceiling," I said.

"That's right. Da Vinci was a genius, and Michelangelo must have been a moron."

"What are you talking about?"

"If he'd used a roller, he could have done it in

four days instead of four years. But back to da Vinci. I know for a fact he did have a way with the ladies."

"Okay, I'm waiting for it, how do you know that?"

"How do you think he met that Mona Lisa lady, and why do you think she's smiling?" He must have seen that I was not amused. "But seriously, you can't expect us to go to a dance club every night. We have to improvise!"

"But these people are spilling their guts in there."

"And where else could we find out so much about them so easily?" he asked. "This goes beyond picking the low-hanging fruit. This is fruit that practically picks itself and jumps into the basket!"

"We've crossed a line here," I said. "We have to go."

"Just walk away?" he asked.

"We can put our heads down and sneak out so nobody notices."

"You don't think they'll notice that we didn't come back?"

"Of course they'll notice, but we won't have to talk to them. Let's just leave."

"That doesn't seem very brave. Where is your integrity?" he asked.

"You're worried about integrity after pulling this?" I could hardly believe my ears.

"Maybe you've helped me to see the light. Maybe this meeting has been a transformational experience for me. In fact, I suggest we walk right back in there and tell them exactly what we've done, admit that we're a couple of frauds who invaded their meeting."

I shook my head. "I'm not sure that's such a good idea either."

"Right, because it's probably the stupidest idea I ever had. Can you imagine how those people would feel if they knew we'd been faking all of this, that we had violated the sanctity of their meeting?"

"They'd feel terrible."

"And even worse, they might feel like they could never trust new people coming into their midst, that they could never be honest or truthful in there again. Can you imagine how much potential damage that could do?"

"I have a pretty good idea, and that's why we shouldn't have come here in the first place," I argued.

"That ship has sailed. What we have to do now is make sure that they never find out what we did. We owe it to them to keep up our story."

"So let me get this straight, you think we should continue to lie, and in lying we're doing them a favour?"

"Exactly, completely, 100 percent correct. Rather than giving them the cold hard truth we're offering them a reassuring lie. Doesn't that make sense?"

Unfortunately, it did.

"I understand how you feel," Ethan said. "And you have my word I won't take you to any place like this again. Okay?"

"Okay, I appreciate that. Thanks."

"No need to thank me. You've taught me something today. Tell you what, you don't have to try to pick up that girl beside you who is so obviously into you."

"She is?"

"No question. We can even slip out now if you want. I do think it would be better to stay till the end of the meeting, but we'll do whatever you decide . . . Well?"

"I'm not sure now."

"Look, if we leave without saying anything, then everybody will take it personally. They'll think it's their fault, something they said or didn't say, and that will produce guilt. And believe me, in a group like this guilt is a pretty strong driving force. They feel guilty about *everything*. I could convince this group that they're responsible for global warming and bad weather. Do you really want to make them feel worse about themselves?"

"Of course not."

"Then let's just go back, finish the meeting, and maybe, just maybe, stick around for a coffee and a couple of cookies. Would that be so wrong?"

"I guess not."

"Good. Let's go back in before somebody gets worried or starts feeling guilty."

It was too late for that. I was already worried and feeling guilty enough for all of us.

CHAPTER EIGHT

We ended up going out with the two girls we'd sat next to at the support group. Ethan had convinced me that we were once again performing a "community service" by allowing them to have a little fun and get away from the "pain of their family situations" for one magical night.

My date, Katie, was sweet and kind, and because I knew her story I felt kind of protective of her. But at the same time, I was feeling guilty about tricking her, and guiltier still for having told all those lies about my mother and father. My father didn't do drugs—he hardly even drank alcohol—and my mother got slightly tipsy when she had more than one glass of white wine. What if, somehow, somebody who knew my family had heard all of that stuff? Then I remembered: in a city this size you could go for years without ever running into anybody you knew. So we went out, and I paid for Katie's movie ticket, bought her an extra-big bag of popcorn, and behaved like a gentleman. As the night went on, I forgot my guilt and really thought I wanted to see her again. But then she started talking about us "going to group together" the following Wednesday, and I realized that I'd have to fake family drug use as an ongoing problem. I wasn't up for that.

I wasn't even sure I was up for another night out with Ethan, but two days later, I found myself at another club, on another Friday night—a different all-ages club from the one we'd gone to the week before. I probably should have stayed home and worked on an assignment that was due on Monday, but it was almost impossible to say no to Ethan. And part of me didn't want to say no. He kept me amused and entertained and occupied. Looking forward to something meant that I didn't have to look back.

I still sometimes woke up in the middle of the night with memories of Jennifer and me rushing back. How could she have done that to me? How could *they* have done that to me? Ethan said a lot of things—he had a theory about everything—and some of it was just plain garbage, but he was right about one thing. Jennifer dumping me didn't hurt nearly as much as Jennifer and Elmer getting together. Tonight, I hoped whatever Ethan had planned would blow away those thoughts and feelings.

The club was hopping, the music was pumping, and dancers swarmed the floor. As always it was almost exclusively girls out there, plus a couple of uncomfortable-looking guys dancing with their dates. There was something so funny about how girls and guys danced differently. Almost without exception, every guy I'd ever seen dance looked wooden. But girls just seemed so natural, and they actually moved to the music in a rhythmic way. I couldn't take my eyes off of them.

A set of fingers snapped right in front of my eyes. I jumped back in my seat. It was Ethan. I hadn't even noticed him reappear.

"What are you doing?" I asked.

"I'm trying to snap you out of your trance."

"What?"

"You've been hypnotized by the girls. Watching them gives you a warm buzz in the back of your head."

"It actually gives me feelings in another part of my body altogether," I said.

"It's the first step to being hypnotized. Before you know it, you'll be squawking like a chicken."

"I thought it was clucking like a chicken."

In response, he just snapped his fingers right in front of my nose again. It was annoying. *He* was annoying.

"No, don't follow the light!" he said. "Listen to my voice! Do not fall into the trap."

"I see a bunch of girls dancing, not a trap."

"Just stay focused and . . . uh-oh. We have to get out of here. We have to leave right now." He had bent over and it looked as if he was trying to hide behind me.

"What's wrong? What are you doing?"

"It's her . . . far side of the dance floor . . . blond hair . . . impossibly high heels . . . beautiful . . . oh, this is bad, she's seen me!"

Almost instantly I saw who he meant. She was beautiful and she was crossing the dance floor, coming toward us, laser eyes locked on Ethan. And she really, really didn't look happy.

"Who is she?" I asked.

"Her name is Mandi, and she signs her name with a little heart over the *i*. I was supposed to go out with her last Saturday night."

"But you were out with me on Saturday."

"That's why I stood her up."

"Why would you do that?"

"I wanted to go out with you instead," he said, and shrugged. "Take it as a compliment."

She moved across the floor. Her expression had gone way beyond angry and right into furious. She looked a little scary. She broke free of the last of the throng of dancers. Trailing behind her was a friend, struggling to keep up. If she'd been a guy, I'd have thought she was coming over to start a fight. And maybe she was!

Almost on cue the song ended.

"Mandi, I'm so glad to see you!" Ethan exclaimed as he got to his feet, opened his arms, and tried to hug her.

She pushed him away. "You are such a jerk, Everett!"

Another false name, of course. I wasn't surprised.

"Jerk . . . I don't understand . . . what's wrong?" Ethan sounded so believable, so genuine, so hurt, as though he'd suddenly forgotten about standing her up. What was he up to?

"You know what you did!" She practically spat out the words.

"I don't know . . . what do you mean?" Ethan looked confused, even shocked. "I'm really looking forward to going out with you tomorrow and—"

"Our date was *last* Saturday! You stood me up! I sat in that restaurant for over an hour, feeling like an idiot, everybody watching me, waiting for you to arrive, and—"

"Wait, wait! Our date is *tomorrow* night, Saturday the twenty-sixth."

"It was last Saturday, the nineteenth, and—"

"Oh, my goodness, I'm so sorry. It's in my phone as the twenty-sixth." He held up his phone as if to offer proof.

"It was *last* Saturday," she said coldly.

"I don't know what to say except to apologize. I feel so awful, so terrible! I made the reservations and I had a whole special night planned and . . . I just don't know what to say!"

She had stopped looking angry, and now she looked confused.

I wasn't confused, but I was impressed. He almost had me believing his story, and I knew for sure it was a complete lie.

"I'm so sorry. Not just because of putting you through all of that, but because I know it means that I lost my chance to go out with somebody as special as you."

Her expression softened slightly. "I was positive it was the nineteenth."

"It's the twenty-sixth. At least, I thought it was. I was telling my cousin all about my plans, all about you. Right?" he said, turning to me for confirmation.

What was I supposed to do? I had to say something. My mind snapped into gear.

"He couldn't shut up about going out with you tomorrow night," I said.

Ethan shot me a look, but then laughed. "Okay, now you're making me seem desperate."

"Not desperate. And I guess now that I've seen you I know why. I thought he had to be exaggerating when he said how beautiful you were."

She looked as though she was blushing a bit as she glanced slightly down.

"Getting the days wrong is not your fault," Ethan said as he put a hand on her shoulder. "It's *my* fault, *my* mistake. I don't know if you can ever forgive me." He paused. "Look, the reservation has been made, it's for tomorrow. It's almost impossible to have the whole thing arranged again for another night, and I know somebody as amazing as you probably already has plans, but do you think that, maybe, you'd be able to . . .?" He let the sentence trail off.

She didn't say yes, but she didn't say no.

"I understand if you can't make it . . . if you don't want to ever see me again. I understand."

"Well . . ."

"It would mean so much to me," he said. "Even more now. I even had something extra-special built into the evening."

"I guess I could go," she said.

"Thank you so much! It means so much that you've forgiven me!"

"'Forgiven' might be going too far. We'll see how special what you have in mind is," she said.

"You won't be disappointed. It will definitely be memorable. Believe me, you will never forget tomorrow night for the rest of your life." He paused. "Perhaps, just as a little extra, we could make it a double date?" Ethan said. "Would your friend be willing to go with you and be my cousin Gary's date?"

I'd been so fascinated—hypnotized—by the scene going on in front of me that I hadn't even glanced at the girl who was with Mandi. She wasn't stunningly beautiful like Mandi, but she was cute. She gave me a shy smile as our eyes met.

"You'd be willing to come along on a date tomorrow night, right?" Mandi asked her.

The girl hesitated. She needed encouragement.

"Believe me, it would be my cousin's honour if you'd go out with him," Ethan said.

I nodded in agreement.

"I guess I could come along," she said.

"But could you change everything to make it for four?" Mandi asked.

"It would be impossible without connections. I have connections," Ethan said. "So?"

"I think we can make it," Mandi said.

"Then it's a date!" Ethan exclaimed. "A double date! Look, we could even start our date tonight, I guess, but my cousin and I have tickets to a concert later on tonight. We were just on our way. It's Gary's favourite band and they were really hard to get, but we could give them up . . ."

"We wouldn't want you to do that!" said my date, whose name I still didn't know. "Please go to the concert." She really did seem sweet.

"Thank you for understanding," I said, gratefully. I had even started thinking about which band I would most want to see in my fantasy world. Somehow with Ethan it seemed possible that we might really be going to a concert.

"No, please, it's all right. We'll see you tomorrow night," Mandi agreed.

Ethan threw his arms around Mandi and gave her a big kiss. She kissed him back. Unbelievable. Somehow he'd managed to get a kiss instead of a punch.

"Thank you so much for agreeing to go out with me again," Ethan said. "I know that you're the sort of girl who wouldn't normally need to give a guy a second chance."

"That's for sure!" she exclaimed. She sounded proud of that.

"I just wish we could stick around for a while and talk but we have to get going, the concert starts in thirty minutes."

He gave, and got, another kiss from Mandi—this one longer and deeper.

"I'm just so lucky that we ran into you tonight or I would have been sitting at the restaurant tomorrow, waiting for you to come, wondering why you weren't there. It would have been terrible," Ethan said.

"It was pretty awful," she said.

"And embarrassing," he added.

She nodded, and actually looked a bit embarrassed just thinking about it.

He gave her one more hug. "Until tomorrow!"

Awkwardly I shook hands with my date. "I'm
looking forward to getting to know you better."

"Me, too," she said. "It's so nice that this all
worked out. See you tomorrow, Gary."

For a split second I'd forgotten that was my name.
I nodded in agreement.

The two girls started back across the dance floor,
Mandi leading the way, the other following in her
wake.

Ethan picked up his Coke and drained it. "Let's
get out of here."

We headed for the exit.

"So, what concert are we not seeing?" I joked.

"Any excuse to get out of there," he said. "That
was pretty tense."

"I can't believe you talked your way out of that. I
almost believed you'd gotten the dates wrong. By the
way, this exclusive restaurant must be expensive."

"Outrageously expensive, and for incredibly small
portions," Ethan said. "I went there with my father a
month ago."

"Just out of curiosity, are we expected to pay for
them?" I didn't mind covering for him but my pockets really weren't that deep.

"Don't be silly, we're not going to pay."

"They're going to pay?"

He shrugged. "Probably not, because they're not
going to get into the restaurant to begin with. It's

really, really hard to get reservations there. I could never get reservations for four for tomorrow."

"But . . . I don't understand."

"It's not like we're going to meet them."

"*What?*"

"I guess I had you fooled too. I didn't want to go out with her last Saturday night and we're not going out with them tomorrow night, either."

"You're joking, right?" I asked.

"No joke. I have better things to do. Besides, didn't you see that it wasn't me she was interested in? She only agreed to go out with me the first time to get into that expensive, exclusive restaurant. Didn't you notice how her whole expression changed when I brought that up again? That girl is a serious snob. She was using me to get what she wanted."

"So why did you agree to go out with her to begin with?" I asked.

"She wanted to use me, so I thought I'd teach her a lesson. Now it's *two* lessons. I'd love to be a fly on the wall at that restaurant when the two of them go in, all dolled up, and realize that we're not going to show up."

I was speechless. Part of me felt sorry for Mandi. A bigger part felt sorry for my date, who was going to be stood up as well. What had she done wrong?

"Look, don't give me those puppy dog eyes of yours. I don't feel guilty, and neither should you," Ethan said.

I did feel guilty—really guilty.

"Just remember, this is all on me. You're just an innocent bystander. You and her friend—she's going to be collateral damage. Did you notice that Mandi didn't introduce her or even ask if she wanted to come along? She just assumed."

I had noticed that.

"Don't feel sorry for Mandi at all. I'm sure she's stood up a few guys in her time. Now, let's get on with the night!"

Part of me wanted to just head home now. The bigger part, maybe not my better part, wanted to see what Ethan had planned for the rest of our night. He was lots of things, but boring wasn't one of them.

CHAPTER NINE

The next five weeks were a crazy ride: from dance clubs to karaoke nights, roller skating, bowling nights, mall trolling, museums and art galleries, church gatherings, and community meetings—although Ethan had kept his word about not going back to special group meetings. We'd even taken our performance to supermarkets! It didn't really matter what we did or where we went—we met girls everywhere. And I was learning from a master. Only time could heal a broken heart, but time spent with other girls seemed to heal it even faster.

One experiment, though, was not turning out to be our most successful.

"I have to apologize," Ethan said. "I thought this might work. And really, it's not like there are many places to go on a Saturday morning."

"Well, it's been different. I've never been to a farmers' market before."

"Neither have I. I saw it as a challenge, but instead it's been a big disappointment," Ethan said.

"The scones and jam were very good, and I did pick up a Christmas present for my mother," I said, holding up the bag that contained the hand-painted silk scarf I'd bought for her. I knew she'd really like it.

Ethan and I had eaten breakfast in a little tent, then we'd wandered through the stalls, checking out the vegetables and fruits, bunches of fresh-cut flowers, jars of preserves and jams, bottles of organic honey, candles and soaps, handmade crafts and clothes and jewellery. Everybody was very friendly—the people at the little snack bar, the people working the stalls, and the customers themselves. Older people and younger couples with kids wandered up and down the aisles, saying "good morning" or offering friendly nods. I also didn't think I'd ever seen so many Birkenstocks in one place before.

"I can't believe you're already buying Christmas presents," Ethan said. "It's still the middle of November. You have plenty of time."

"It's sort of a thing in my family. It's like a contest to see who can give the best presents," I explained.

"Did you do the same thing with what's her name?"

It was one of the few things I didn't like about Ethan—that needle that he'd poke me with from time to time.

Last year I'd given Jennifer a chain and pendant, and she was so happy that . . . I caught myself mid-thought, mid-emotion. I wondered if she still wore it. Part of me wanted to ask for it back, but it wasn't like it was an engagement ring. I'd given it to her, and she could do whatever she wanted with it. She could even wear it when she was out with Elmer. I knew he liked it because he'd helped me pick it out. That made me sad and angry at the same time.

"Well?" he asked.

"I do that for *everybody*, including her."

"Well, in that case, I'm looking forward to something really special from you," he said.

"Do you want a scarf too?" I asked. "Because I could go back and get you one just like my mother's."

"I don't think there's anything in this market that I want picked up for me. We should just call it quits."

Ethan had picked me up at 7:30 that morning, much earlier than I would have liked on a Saturday, especially after another late Friday night. We'd gone to an art show opening at a gallery. That had been another first for me, but as always we'd met some girls. They were students at an arts college, and they were very . . . different. Actually, I'd found them a little bit frightening.

My parents were beginning to be concerned about how often I was going out. They hadn't said anything, but I could tell. My marks had dropped a little, and they were worried that I wasn't devoting enough time to school, especially with college applications coming up.

Ethan was feeling restless. He kept looking around, then checking his phone. "I've wasted your time. And, more important, I've wasted *my* time."

I was in no particular hurry to go. There were some things here that kind of reminded me of home. The place had a kind of a small-town feel—everyone seemed to know everyone else, and nobody was in a hurry. In the city it felt as though everybody was always in a rush.

"I sort of like being here," I said.

"Look, I screwed up. No need to try to make me feel better."

"I wasn't. Besides, there are a few 'potentials' here," I said, using his own word.

"Nothing worth getting out of bed at seven in the morning for," he said, "unless I was trying to get away before somebody else woke up. But I admire your positive outlook and determination. So, you lead and I'll follow."

We wound our way back through the stalls, passing the families and seniors. I had noticed a group of three girls before—Ethan had passed them by without even giving them a second glance—and there they were, standing around a booth selling organic vegetables and kale chips. They were all about our age, and sort of pretty in a makeup-limited, casual, hair-pulled-back kind of way. They reminded me of girls from back home.

Actually, as we got closer I realized that one of them was very pretty, even though she wasn't doing anything to draw attention to it. She wore jeans, a white T-shirt, and sandals with socks, but she was making it work. If she was wearing makeup, I couldn't tell. Around her neck was a scarf, very similar to the one I'd just bought for my mother.

"How about them?" I said.

"First off, there are three of them and two of us," Ethan said.

"I did the math."

"Did you? And do you also realize that a five and two twos does not make a nine?"

I knew which one he thought was the five. "She's at least a seven," I protested.

"She loses two points for her choice of footwear." He shrugged. "Are you using the Hicksville scale again?"

"It's Woodstock, and no."

"Okay, well, if you want to lower yourself, who am I to argue? Let's go for it. Do you have a plan in mind?"

"I was sort of counting on you," I said.

"Not me. I'm not wasting my talent on them. Besides, you've had weeks to absorb and observe, so let's see what you've learned."

"Challenge accepted," I said.

Slowly I wandered over to where they stood, while Ethan hung back. They were so occupied that they didn't even notice me eavesdropping on their conversation. I stared at the organic vegetables, listening and picking up on a couple of their names: Emma and Rachel. The third one, the one Ethan had called a five, remained nameless. And then she said something about kale being "overrated" and I plunged right in.

"Excuse me," I said. "I couldn't help but hear that you think kale is overrated. I happen to love kale. Could you explain to me what's wrong with kale?"

She looked up at me, clearly taken by surprise. The surprised expression changed as she looked at me—looked right into my eyes. It was like she was trying to figure me out, as if she was appraising me, and I had to work not to look away. She had beautiful blue eyes, with little flecks of gold.

She shrugged. "It's just that it's everywhere. In salads, as snack food, in smoothies even."

"But it is healthy."

"No more than broccoli or collards, cabbage or bok choy," she said. I had no idea what bok choy even was. It sounded like a lead actor in a kung fu movie. "And all of those are tastier and less tough. Kale needs to be cooked longer, and that leeches out a lot of the nutrients," she explained.

"I hadn't thought of that. You really know your stuff," I said.

"I like to know what goes into my body," she said.

"You are what you eat," I offered. Okay, that was bad. I had to add something. "That was a big part of why I was asking. I'm always looking for new things to supplement my diet."

"You're a vegetarian?" one of the others—Rachel—asked.

I almost blurted out that I thought bacon was nature's perfect food before I realized, from the little that had been said, that this girl with the blue eyes and gold flecks was probably a vegetarian. I hoped my expression hadn't given it away. There was only one safe response.

"I've been a vegetarian for almost a year." I quickly

glanced over at Ethan, who gave a small nod. "But I can't believe how many people would rather I just started eating meat again."

The nameless girl laughed—a nice laugh, not bitter or mocking. "It's not easy sometimes," she said. Bingo—got that one right! She was a vegetarian. "I get that sort of comment from my mother and father, and sometimes even some of my friends," she said.

One of the girls—the one named Emma—looked embarrassed. "Sorry."

The girl reached out to her friend. "I didn't mean that the way it sounded," she said. "You are one of the kindest, sweetest people I know."

"I've tried to change my eating habits to become a vegetarian. I just can't keep it up. It's not my fault," Emma said.

"Bacon?" I asked, remembering something I'd read somewhere. "It's bacon that keeps calling you back, right?"

"Bacon," she said, shaking her head. "It's so tempting."

"It's amazing how many names they have for meat," the nameless one said. "Bacon, pork, ham, tenderloin, or ribs, it's still pig, but they don't want to use that word because we might realize we're eating an animal that was once a living, breathing creature."

"It's the same as calling it veal, beef, and hamburger so people don't think about eating a cow," I said.

"Exactly!" she exclaimed. "And they both have high levels of social intelligence," she added.

Social intelligence . . . what exactly did that even mean? I strained my brain, trying to think of anything and everything I knew about being a vegetarian. Ethan, standing just off to one side, looked amused. I wasn't sure if that was because he thought I was doing well or because he found my efforts amusingly amateurish.

"Okay, how's this for lack of support," I said. "My doctor doesn't believe in me being a vegetarian. During my annual physical last month he kept going on and on about how humans were designed to eat meat."

"I've heard all those arguments too," she said. "All that talk about canine teeth and how if we were meant to be vegetarians we'd have two stomachs, like cows."

I suddenly remembered something I'd heard in the car with my mother a couple of weeks earlier. She was always listening to these *Radiolab* podcasts. This one was going to be really helpful.

"It's more than biology; it's about morality. Putting aside the whole issue of animal rights—"

"And that's a big issue," she said.

"Yes, of course, but there's a bigger human rights issue involved."

Rachel turned to Emma. "Doesn't he sound just like Raine?"

Before I could ask how I sounded like the weather, the nameless girl laughed. "He does sound like me."

So that was her name—Raine. That was so fitting and so funny that I almost laughed out loud. No wonder she was a vegetarian—her parents were probably flat-out hippies. I figured it could have been worse—she could have been Grain or Apple or Granola. I instantly decided I needed a name that sounded hippie-ish but not too bizarre.

"By the way, my name is Dakota." I only wished I could have thought of something that started with the letter G. I knew Ethan would be disappointed.

The three girls introduced themselves to me. I motioned for Ethan to join us. "And this is my friend." I thought about his name. I wanted something to throw him. "His name is Orion."

"Like the constellation?" Emma asked.

"Like the constellation," Ethan said, not missing a beat.

He shook hands with all three of the girls as they introduced themselves.

"We were going to go over to the tent to have a coffee," Ethan said.

"Only if it's organic, fair-trade coffee, of course," I added.

"It is," Emma said.

"Would you three like to join us?" I asked.

Raine looked at her watch. "I guess we could for a while. Then I've got to go to Pig Island."

"Pig Island?" Ethan asked. "Is that in the Caribbean?"

They all laughed, and I was glad it was Ethan who'd asked the question. He didn't look very happy about it. He was used to people laughing with him, not at him.

"It's not really an island," Emma said.

"It *is* an island," Rachel said. "It's a traffic island."

Now I felt as confused as Ethan.

"I'll explain it to you two over coffee," Raine said.

CHAPTER TEN

After the five of us had got our coffees and talked for a bit, Ethan—a.k.a. Orion—took Rachel and Emma away to help him search for a present for his "sister" for "her birthday tomorrow." I figured he got that idea because they had all been so impressed that I'd bought something for my mother. Of course, Ethan didn't have a sister, but he was doing me a solid favour by taking the other girls away and letting me spend time with Raine. He was a good friend that way.

I was enjoying our conversation. Raine—she explained that her name was spelled with the *e* at the end—was very determined, very smart, and really didn't seem to care what I thought. She just spoke the truth as she saw it. Not that she wanted to be offensive, she just had strong beliefs. Her passion was infectious, and I had to admit that I felt jealous. I was mirroring her belief system, agreeing with what she was saying, but that was all I had—empty words. She was committed, and I was just, well, doing a good job of faking it.

While she spoke I looked her over. She was definitely not a five, and even to call her a seven would have been an injustice. She didn't wear much makeup, her hair was held together in a simple ponytail, and her T-shirt was unassuming, unrevealing, and, I assumed, made with natural fibres. It was as far from designer as you could possibly get. Her only jewellery was a small beaded bracelet on one wrist and a watch on the other.

She wasn't hiding anything. How strange, she wasn't hiding anything about herself, and I was hiding everything. She kept talking and I kept asking her questions, partly because Ethan had taught me that girls like it when you ask questions, and partly because it was easier than making up things about myself that I'd have to remember later.

Like me, Raine was a high school senior. She had a younger brother named Steve. Thank goodness his name wasn't Sleet or Snow or I couldn't have handled it. She wanted to go away for university next year. She was hoping ultimately to get into medicine, because she saw it as the best way to "make a difference." She'd given it a lot of thought. I figured she gave everything a lot of thought.

"Are you going straight into college after you graduate, or are you taking some time off?" she asked.

I tried to think about what Dakota would want to be, what she'd want me to be if I was going to mirror

ERIC   WALTERS

her response, and what I wanted to be. I should have just said that pre-med fascinated me, but instead I said, "I'm not sure."

"It's probably better to be undecided than go running off in the wrong direction," she said.

"I've never really thought of it that way, but you're right. Could you talk to my parents?"

"Are you asking me home to meet your family?" she asked.

She looked so serious for a minute that I started to sputter. "No, I was just—"

She burst out laughing. "Got ya! How about you join me on Pig Island today instead?"

Raine had told me more about Pig Island, which was essentially a traffic island on Lakeshore Avenue that trucks had to pass on their way to the slaughter-house. There was a traffic light there, and Raine and some others would be there when they stopped and waited for the light to change. I asked what they did, and she replied that they were there to "bear witness," to let people, and the pigs themselves, know that they were aware of what was going on. She explained that the truck had little ventilation holes in the sides and the pigs would be pressed up against them, and that sometimes you could see their snouts or eyes peering through. Sometimes they talked to the pigs, and other times they tried to speak to the drivers, most of whom, she said, tried to ignore them. Apparently there were sometimes incidents when the truck drivers got angry and yelled at people, but Raine had never seen that happen.

"How many people are usually there protesting?"
I asked.

"It varies. Some days there are only a few of us,
but sometimes there are twenty or more."

"It sounds intense," I said.

"It can be. Do you have a dog?"

"Not any more. Lola, our standard poodle, died
about six months ago."

"I'm sorry. And I can still hear it in your voice
that it bothers you," she said.

"How could it not bother you? She was a part of
our family for nine years." I felt a little catch in my
throat. "She was a good dog."

Losing Lola had hurt. I'd tried to convince myself
that she was just a dog, but she was my dog, our dog.
And I'd been missing her more since we'd moved
than I had right after she died. We'd been talking
about getting a new dog, but I think my father was
still a little raw over her loss, and that's why he wanted
to wait until the spring. He was a big guy but he had
an even bigger heart.

"And those pigs are smarter than your dog."

"I did mention she was a poodle, right?" I said.

"I know they're smart dogs."

"The smartest. It was like she could tell when
somebody wasn't feeling well or had had a bad day,"
I said.

"Dogs possess both emotional and social intelligence," she said. "Just like cows and, of course, pigs.
They think and they feel and they care about the
members of their herd or pack."

"'If you prick us, do we not bleed?'" I asked.

Without missing a beat she replied, "'If you tickle us, do we not laugh?'"

"'If you poison us, do we not die?'" I said, adding the next line.

"I don't usually have people quote Shakespeare to me," Raine said. She looked impressed and surprised all at once.

"I don't usually have people quote lines back to me, either. *The Merchant of Venice* is pretty powerful."

She didn't answer right away. She looked as though she was considering her words. I got the feeling she did that a lot. She was thinking and I was looking. She was beautiful and obviously smart. I figured she also had emotional and social intelligence. Even more than a pig. I almost chuckled, wondering if she'd take that as an insult or a compliment.

"Please don't get me wrong," she said slowly. "I know that *The Merchant of Venice* is about prejudice and racism against humans. I appreciate that human life is sacred, but still, on many levels, life is life. Those willing to show cruelty to animals are willing to show cruelty to other people."

"I think I'd really like to go to Pig Island some time," I said. "Do you go every Saturday?"

"It's usually every Wednesday. Today is special. You're welcome to come along, if you'd like," she said.

"I'd like that . . . but I can't today. Eth . . . either way, it would be great if my friend came along too." I'd almost slipped up by blurting out Ethan's name, but I'd sort of covered it. What was his fake name? . . . Oh yeah. "Orion has other plans for us for today, and I don't want to disappoint him."

"I understand. There'll be other times, if you really want to come."

She'd slightly emphasized "really," as though she had doubts about whether I was sincere. I was. I was also pretty sure Ethan wouldn't want to have anything to do with it.

"I do want to come. Do I just show up?"

"That's all. Hopefully I'll be there when you do," she said.

If she wasn't there, I thought, then I'd just leave.

Ethan reappeared with Emma and Rachel. They were laughing at something that he'd said. They both looked thrilled to be with him. I just wished they'd all stayed away longer.

"I've really enjoyed our conversation," I said.

"Actually, so have I," she said.

"You sound surprised."

She shrugged. "I guess I am."

"I'm not sure if I should be insulted or complimented."

"Maybe a little of both. We have to get going now," she said.

As Raine got up, I drained the last of my coffee and we joined the group. Emma and Rachel were rather taken with Ethan. No surprise. He seemed to have that effect on females. Actually, he had that effect on most people. Whatever he was selling, though, Raine didn't seem to be buying it. Her expression was at best skeptical, certainly not amused or enchanted.

Was that because he wasn't aiming his charm at her? Or was it something else? Was she seeing through him, or was she somehow immune to him?

"It really was a pleasure to meet you," Raine said.

"You too." Awkwardly I offered her my hand and we shook. Okay, that didn't show much social intelligence. How did pigs say goodbye?

Ethan and the other two girls hugged—should I have gone in for a hug with Raine?—and then the three of them were gone, disappearing behind some stalls.

"That was pretty exciting," Ethan said. "I saw that you got a nice, *firm* handshake. Was that good for you?"

"I think a handshake from a seven is better than hugs from a couple of twos," I snapped, and instantly felt bad for saying that about them.

"Point taken, although I'll still argue about her being a seven."

Now I was feeling a little annoyed, and protective of Raine. I tried not to show either.

"I guess a hug would have been better, but I'm no 'Orion.' Those two were pretty impressed by you."

"What else would you expect? I'm way out of their league," he said.

Now I was just plain irritated and didn't bother to hide it. "You don't know that for sure."

He gave me a questioning look. "Of course I do. If you did a quantification of *my* attributes and *their* attributes it would be clear that I have a far higher numeric value. They were, at best, a four."

THE ART OF PICKING UP GIRLS

"I thought they were twos," I said.

"That's rather cruel of you to say."

"It was *you* who said it!"

"Two, three, four, or even a five or six—what does it matter? They are definitely below a nine, which is what I am."

"Not a ten?"

"That would be a little conceited, don't you think? Look, I'm just being realistic. I'm bright, I get relatively good marks despite my lack of effort, friendly, verbal, I have money, I'm well-dressed, and have a wonderful flashy car—"

"You count your car and clothes into the equation?"

"You can count lots of things in. Admit it, aren't you impressed by my car?"

"It is nice," I agreed.

"And, of course, I am *really* good-looking."

"No ego issues here."

"Not ego. Just a fact. I have a mirror. I'm classically good-looking in a way that females find attractive. You're not bad yourself."

"This is getting a little uncomfortable."

"Don't be stupid. Don't *you* think I'm very attractive?"

"I guess I've just never thought of—"

"Don't be a liar as well. We're all continually judging each other by things like our looks. I'm really good-looking. You are also good-looking, not quite at my level, but close. Now, did she at least give you her phone number?" Ethan asked.

"Oh . . . I forgot to ask her."

"It doesn't matter. No question you could have got it. We'll count that as a given. Besides, you'll forget all about her by the end of tonight. Do you know what I have planned?"

"I never know what you have planned," I said.

"Let me just say that you're going to have two of the best dates of your life."

"Two?"

"Not enough? You were hoping for three?" he asked.

"I'm good with one . . . although two might make me twice as happy."

"Then you, my friend, are going to be very, very happy. Let's get out of here before you see another girl who's a waste of our time."

CHAPTER ELEVEN

I did a quick crossover, drew the ball back, and put up a shot. It hit the rim, bounced to the side, and started rolling back down the driveway toward me.

"Nice shot."

I turned around. Ethan was standing there. His car was on the street. I hadn't seen him pull up or walk over.

"Everybody misses," I said.

"Some more than others."

He held out his hands and I passed him the ball. He rolled it around in his hands, bounced it a couple of times, and then put up a shot—nothing but net!

"That was impressive," I said as I retrieved the ball.

"You're easily impressed."

I threw it back to him and he quickly put up a shot. Slightly off, it bounced high off the rim and dropped in.

"That one was just lucky," I said, running after the ball again.

"They both count for three points. Let's shoot for a bit. It feels nice to have a basketball back in my hands."

I tossed him the ball and he started dribbling it. He put the ball left to right and through his legs, drawing it back and forth. He was good.

"So, what do you think about last night?" Ethan asked.

"Unbelievable. You did it." Ethan had promised me not one but two dates and, as usual, he did not disappoint.

"Which part did you like best?"

"That party was a nice place to start," I said.

"And those two girls were certainly hot. I've got them on file in my phone."

Ethan made notes on his phone about our dates. That was good, because without those notes we could never have kept our dates, and more importantly our stories, straight.

"Did you notice how saying we had to leave the party made them want us even more?" he asked.

"I don't think they're used to guys walking away from them."

"Human nature," he said. "You want what you can't have."

He passed to me and I dribbled across the key and put up "my" shot—a short hook. It dropped. Thank goodness.

"Old-school baby hook. I like that," he said as he

picked up the rolling ball. "We really didn't have a choice, given that we had that other date to get to."

"*Two* other dates," I said.

"You did sort of imply that you were hoping for three, so I did what I could. It ended up being like our own little version of speed-dating."

We'd left the party because Ethan had arranged for us to take another two girls out for dinner. We ate, had some fun, and then we left those two behind and met up with Jennifer and Sierra, the girls we'd picked up at the mall. This was sort of our third date with them— we'd gone out with them again about three weeks after we'd first met them. It was strange, but I'd almost forgotten about them.

The hardest part for me was remembering names. Not just their names, but our names. Ethan seemed terribly amused by the whole thing. He loved what he called "the game, the theatre, the drama." Between the time we waved and the time we hugged hello, Ethan would have to remind me of *our* names. How strange, to have to be told your own name.

"So, I'm assuming you liked the after-dinner date better," he said.

"I liked them both, but Jennifer and Sierra were just so thrilled that we'd come all the way down from Buck Lake to see them it was like we could do no wrong," I said.

"It's all about setting up the scenario. Think about it. If they knew we lived only a few miles away and hadn't seen them for weeks between dates, wouldn't they be upset with us?"

"Definitely."

"And instead they felt complimented, honoured, thrilled. They believe we truly care for them."

"I *do* like Jennifer," I said.

"Graham, you like *everybody.*"

"That's not true."

"Isn't it? When you saw Jennifer last night did you even recognize her right away?"

"Well . . . we've met a lot of girls, and it was a while ago."

"It wasn't that long and it isn't that many."

"Twenty-seven," I said.

"You're counting?" he asked.

"Aren't you?"

"Of course. I keep track of everything, but that's more of an accounting practice than anything else. My guess is that you'd be willing to seriously date any one of the girls we've met along the way. Heck, you even liked what's her name from the farmers' market."

"Raine."

I put up another shot, just outside the three, and it missed. Ethan got the rebound but kept any comment to himself. What I didn't want him to know was that I had been thinking about Raine a lot. Even during last night's dates, and, to be honest, this morning, too. I'd mentioned her to my parents over breakfast.

"Yeah, whatever," he said, shaking his head. "I could never date anybody named after a weather system."

"This coming from a guy whose last name is Frost?" I asked.

"Point taken, but that's my *last* name. What if my parents had named me Jack?"

I couldn't help but chuckle. That was the thing about Ethan, even when he was confusing, or annoying, or even out-and-out wrong, he was still always amusing.

"Seriously, though, what were her parents thinking when they hung that handle on her?"

"I guess they were looking for unique."

"Unique and pathetic are close neighbours. Maybe the two of you *should* date. Who knows where it might lead? Eventually you could get married and live in a commune. She'll teach yoga and you'll become a baker of bread made from ancient grains and you'll have a couple of daughters named Drizzle and Downpour."

"First off, it would be gluten-free bread I'd bake, and second, I think our children would be called Misty and Precipitation," I said, and he laughed.

"Nice to see you know this is ridiculous."

"Her name is a bit out there, but she was pretty and nice and smart."

"She wasn't that pretty, and she certainly wasn't very nice to me," Ethan said.

"She was nice to me. Maybe she's perceptive enough to see through you."

"Now that hurts. And she wasn't especially nice to you, either. You are *so* easy. I, on the other hand, have very discerning standards."

"Discerning? You find somebody to date everywhere we go."

"That's because I'm a very giving person."

I noticed something then. "You're in the same clothes you were wearing when you dropped me off last night."

"That's because I didn't go home last night. Not counting the girls at the party, you had two dates. After I dropped you off I went out on a third. I came here straight from there."

"Unbelievable! So, where did you meet her and what's her name?"

"You don't know her. You remember that call I got last night? The one where I excused myself and left you with the girls at dinner? She called to tell me her parents were out of town for the night and she was feeling a 'little afraid' of being alone. I made sure she had nothing to fear."

"How heroic of you."

"That's me, a regular Spider-Man. So, are you ready to go?" Ethan asked.

"It's Sunday morning," I said. "Are we going to church?"

"Of course not . . . although that does give me an idea I might want to try out some day."

"I've got some school work to catch up on," I said.

"That, my friend, is a poor excuse. You'll have tonight to do that. Let's go."

As always, it was almost impossible to say no.

"Should I change?" I asked.

"No, you look adorable in a sweaty, smelly, kind of grungy way." He bounced me the ball. "Um . . . I was thinking . . . do you have a pair of basketball shoes and some shorts I can borrow? I was thinking about a little game of one-on-one before we go . . . unless you're afraid . . ."

"Of you?" I scoffed. "I'm pretty good, you know."

"Maybe small-town, Hicksville good. I'm big-city good."

"So you're saying the Theory of Relativity applies to basketball as well as girls?" I asked.

"I'm always impressed when you apply my logic. It lets me know that my teaching hasn't gone completely to waste. So, you think you can handle a little beat-down?"

Typical Ethan.

"I guess we're about to find out which one of us is the hammer and which is the nail," I said.

He smiled, and mimed holding a hammer and hitting a nail. Well, we'd soon see who had the hammer.

"Thank you," I said, as the waitress put down another platter of pancakes.

I felt downright Hobbit-like eating my second breakfast, but I was really hungry after playing basketball. I grabbed a couple of the pancakes and put them on my plate. I wasn't going to wait for Ethan, who was circulating through the restaurant. I was more interested in the food, and he was more interested in the people eating the food at the other tables and booths.

We'd played two games of one-on-one. I'd won the first and he'd won the second, and we'd agreed not to play a third. We were a pretty even match. He was slicker and had better moves, and I was stronger and tougher in the paint. I thought that summed us both up nicely.

My sister and father had come out to watch partway through the first game. My dad was cheering for me and Olivia for Ethan. I thought maybe she had a little crush on him. I also knew I'd personally crush his head if he ever thought about dating her.

After the game we'd both cleaned up before coming here to eat. It was a gigantic restaurant that specialized in breakfast. There must have been a hundred different tables, and people came and went pretty fast, so there were always new customers—or, as Ethan called them, new "potentials."

Ethan returned and plopped down across from me. "I eavesdropped. Their names are Rebecca and Sarah, and they're sitting by the front window."

I looked past the pancakes and past Ethan to the far side of the room, partially blocked by some latticework dividers.

"You can probably see Sarah, she's facing us, but Rebecca has her back to us. Classic example of the Best-Friend Syndrome."

That was another of Ethan's endless theories. According to the Best-Friend Syndrome, the more stunning one girl is, the plainer her best friend needs to be. I had told him that I thought it was just a variation on the Theory of Relativity, but he argued that it was a completely different theory, and that sometimes he felt like he was trying to explain quantum physics to a chimpanzee. Good thing I liked chimpanzees, or I might have taken offence.

It was hard to keep up with all his theories. He had one about first names, one about tattoos and the places those tattoos were located, theories about girls raised without fathers and girls raised with stepfathers, theories about hair colour and makeup styles, whether they smoked or not, the types of music they listened to, and whether or not they liked romantic comedies. In fact, he told me that if I'd been a girl he would have dated me based on the fact that I like chick flicks, which would make me an easy mark. I wasn't sure whether I should have found that disturbing or reassuring— which actually made it even more disturbing.

At one point I'd thought he was just making this stuff up on the fly, but I'd learned that he wasn't. He actually sat down and thought all these theories through. I couldn't help but wonder what he might have accomplished if he'd put this much effort into school, or sports, or learning to play an instrument . . . or world peace. He probably could have talked people into world peace—assuming, that is, that it was a completely female audience.

"So what do you think?" he asked.

Sarah did look attractive enough from a distance. And although I really couldn't see anything except the other girl's back she certainly had nice-looking hair and fancy earrings.

"Rebecca is dressed expensively, she spends a lot of time on her hair, and her makeup is a bit overdone for the daytime," he said.

"You know way too much about makeup."

"Should a deer hunter know about camo?" he asked.

"Not a good example since the hunter wears the camo, and we're not hunting."

"Yes we are, except with us, it's strictly catch-and-release. Oh, and then we run away and hide so they can't find us."

"So the one with her back to us, Rebecca, is obviously the one you're going to want to end up with," I said.

"Of course, but this is going to be tough and I'll need your help."

"Not to be difficult or uncooperative, but knowing you the way I do, I need to know what exactly you want me to do before I agree to it. What's your plan?"

"We're both going to try to pick up the other one, Sarah," Ethan said.

"Okay, now that's just confusing me."

"Exactly! That's the plan . . . to confuse them! We're going to get them lost in a little theory I call the Fog of War. I wasn't sure you were ready for it until now. This one is pretty complex. In a classic war situation, the participants, the soldiers, become uncertain what to do when new and unexpected situations arise. They can't see things clearly, and instead they view the world as if through a thick fog."

"I think I've actually heard of that. And just how does it apply here?"

"We're going to produce uncertainty to confuse our enemy."

"I thought they were our prey?"

"Now you're splitting semantic hairs. We're both going to talk to Sarah, laugh at her jokes, ask her

THE ART OF PICKING UP GIRLS

questions, offer to get her a drink, look at her, and focus on her to the complete and utter exclusion of Rebecca."

I laughed. "I get it. Rebecca is not going to expect that at all."

"Neither of them will, and Rebecca is going to *hate* it. She'll be shocked, confused, and possibly even angry. She will be lost in the fog of war."

"Maybe she'll just be happy for her friend," I said.

He snorted dismissively. "We will continue to ignore Rebecca, no matter what she says or how she responds. We'll act as if she doesn't exist. And, whatever you do, do not, I repeat, *do not* look into her eyes. Do not even look directly at her, or your resolve will be weakened and she will read that. Do you think you can handle it?"

"I can try," I said.

"Trying isn't good enough. You have to do it. Then, at the right moment—and I will determine that moment—you will win the battle for fair Sarah and I will, as consolation, allow myself to be with Rebecca."

"And I'm stuck with Sarah."

"That sounds so crude, so chauvinistic. You are looking at a girl across a restaurant and making judgments about her soul, about her intrinsic value, based entirely on her physical appearance. I expected better of you."

"It does sound terribly shallow. Now, who does that remind me of?" I said.

"Clearly you need to associate with a finer group of people. Perhaps, beneath the surface, Sarah is the catch, and I will end up stuck with the egocentric, shallow, vain girl who proves that beauty is only skin deep." He stopped and smiled. "Thank goodness that's as deep as I'm prepared to look. Well?"

"I'm in. After all, it's not like I don't owe you."

"You already look like you're having second thoughts," he said.

If I was, it was because the plan called for us to be pretty mean to both the girls, letting Sarah think we were totally into her when we weren't, and then freezing out Rebecca. With some of the other girls Ethan had targeted, we'd known they were stuck-up or mean or selfish before we moved in, and I could tell myself they were just getting what they deserved. These two might be perfectly nice girls. But I was pretty sure Ethan would mock me if I tried to make that point.

"I was just wondering if it will work," I said instead.

"It'll work. Have I ever been wrong before? The only thing that could mess up this plan is . . . well, it's you," Ethan said.

"Me?"

With Ethan there always had to be that little taunt. I was pretty sure he did it just to motivate me. I knew it was coming, but it worked every time.

"I guess we'll see if *you* can pull it off," I told him.

"I'm ready. Just try not to screw it up."

We finished up our pancakes quickly and Ethan insisted on paying. He put down a wad of cash that included a hefty tip for our waitress. He always left a big tip, and he wasn't just being showy. He really liked being generous to people.

I followed behind him as we walked toward the front door—toward the two girls. He stopped directly in front of them. I had a pretty good idea how he'd start this since he knew their names.

"Sarah, it's me," Ethan said. "Evan."

I couldn't help but smile. I got it right.

She looked a little confused. "Of course . . . hi, Evan."

"You really don't remember me, do you? Be honest. It's okay," Ethan said.

"I'm so sorry." She did look genuinely sorry.

"Please, don't be. You must meet so many guys, and I know they'd never forget you, but you might forget them. I get it."

Now she looked a little shocked and a lot pleased.

"But I'm not going to let you off easy. Maybe you'll still remember where we met . . . But where are my manners? This is my friend, Gavin."

"I'm pleased to meet you." I took her hand with both hands, shook, and stared directly into her eyes. She did have pretty brown eyes, and there was friendliness behind them.

"This is my friend, Rebecca," she said.

"Nice to meet you," I said, still holding Sarah's hand and not even turning to look at Rebecca.

"Yeah, hello, Rebecca," Ethan said, without turning toward her either.

"Do you eat here very often?" Sarah asked. I figured she was fishing around for clues about where she knew "Evan" from.

"It's one of my favourite places, but I had to drag Gavin here this morning."

"And I'm glad he did," I said. "The food was

good . . . but now that I've met Sarah I see the real attraction."

I had to prove to Ethan that I was more than capable of playing this game, and that cheesy statement was aimed directly at him.

"You didn't actually say that, did you?" Ethan exclaimed.

"I said it and I meant it," I said. "Why? Don't you think so too?"

"Not that I disagree, I just can't believe you could be that bold."

Sarah looked incredibly pleased. Maybe I shouldn't have worried. What was wrong with making her happy?

"Would you like to join us?" Sarah asked.

"We've eaten, but we could have another coffee," Ethan suggested.

I sat down beside Sarah before he could and he sat down beside Rebecca. I noticed that he left lots of space between them and he didn't even glance in her direction. I turned in my seat so that I was looking almost directly at Sarah, with Rebecca in my peripheral vision.

The conversation continued, focused entirely on Sarah. Repeatedly, either Sarah tried to deflect attention to Rebecca—which was what she would have expected to happen normally—or Rebecca tried to burst in. We wouldn't let her. I thought at some point she'd just get up and walk away, but she didn't. Maybe she couldn't. The more we worked to ignore her, the harder she worked to not be ignored. Once again,

Ethan and his theory seemed to be right. This was a contest, and since she didn't have a clue it existed, we had a distinct advantage.

As planned, I stayed focused on Sarah, but I couldn't help stealing an occasional glance at Rebecca. Strangely, as it went on, Sarah did start to seem more attractive and Rebecca less. It obviously wasn't anything physical as much as it was the effect of confidence. Confidence, I'd learned, was critical. Ethan was living proof of that—he just oozed confidence, and people responded to it. Was it biological? Did desperation smell one way and confidence another?

The whole thing, this social experiment, was amusing me more than I would have imagined. Not just because this was panning out the way Ethan had outlined it, but because I thought that maybe, on some level, it would be good for Rebecca to not always be the belle of the ball. Maybe it was all right for Sarah to feel that, and for Rebecca to feel what Sarah usually felt. I got the feeling that a little burst of humility might be good for her. After all, she was showing no sign whatsoever of being happy for her friend's sudden popularity.

"Sarah, would you like something from the dessert bar?" I asked.

"I was just going to ask her that!" Ethan protested.

"You snooze, you lose." I turned back to Sarah. "How about if you come with me and we get something?"

She smiled demurely. "I'd like that."

I got up and offered her my hand and helped her to her feet. For a split second I thought that I had actually "won." I'd been involved in fooling myself. But instead, according to the objective of the game, I was going to walk away with second prize, leaving Ethan to capture the trophy. Really, though, it wasn't that bad. For me, this was about more than just picking up a couple of girls. It was about having a friend, somebody to have fun with, somebody to help me forget what had happened to me.

I should have been thinking about Sarah, but as we walked away all I could think of was Raine. Why hadn't I got her phone number? The only other way to find her again was to head down to that Pig Island, on my own, and hope she'd be there.

CHAPTER TWELVE

Once again, going back to school on Monday was a lot harder than I'd have liked. I was supposed to meet Ethan at the end of the day but I had an unexpected delay—I'd fallen asleep in my last class, and then continued to doze for an additional fifteen minutes after class was dismissed. I'd woken to an empty room, feeling disturbed and a little disoriented. The teacher had obviously been "kind enough" not to wake me when he left.

Falling asleep in class was no surprise. I'd spent most of Sunday evening and well into the night catching up on school work, especially an assignment for English that was due. I'd never missed handing in an assignment in my life, but I'd been up so late finishing it that I'd slept in, almost been late for first period, dragged around the school all day, and had to fight not to drift off in most of my classes.

I hurried through the emptying halls, hoping Ethan hadn't got fed up and left. We were supposed to meet in front of the school. I'd already pulled out my phone but there were so many dead spots in the halls that I hadn't been able to get through. The same way I didn't like to miss deadlines, I didn't like to keep people waiting—it was inconsiderate.

"Hey, Graham!"

I spun around. It was Glenn. He was dressed for basketball. They practised every night they didn't have a game. He was soaked with sweat and was standing by the drinking fountain outside the gym. I could hear the sound of squeaking shoes on the gym floor.

"How are you doing?" I asked.

"Not bad, but not great. Coach is working us hard after Friday's loss."

"It was a tough game. I thought you deserved to win."

"Coach thought so too. Glad you came. I figure you and Ethan must be out having some adventures."

"Adventure is almost his middle name . . . but you'd know that."

Glenn had always been friendly with me but I had the feeling he was holding back. I couldn't help thinking that he felt a little jealous of me. After all, I was kind of taking his place. I wondered how much he knew already and how much I should tell him. I didn't want him to feel any worse.

"Yeah, we had some good times. I miss those adventures . . . well, sometimes . . ."

I looked at him in surprise. And it made me think—there was one thing I wanted to check on, even if I wasn't sure I was going to like the answer.

"I guess when the basketball season is over you'll be back working as Ethan's wingman," I said.

"Yeah, I'm sure we'll go out some, you know, maybe all of us and some of the other guys, but I think that spot belongs to you now."

"Oh, I thought you'd want it back," I said.

He shook his head. "Don't get me wrong, Ethan's my buddy, he's a great guy, and we had some great times together," Glenn said. "It's just that being around him can be tiring."

I laughed. "I know. He doesn't seem to have an off switch."

"And when you're around him, you can't have one either." He paused and looked as though he was thinking something through before he spoke. "Being around Ethan is almost like being on a drug."

"What do you mean?"

"Ethan is like a high. He always has something planned, a new adventure, a new scheme, a new rule or theory he wants to try out."

"Okay, I do get that."

"But he's also addictive. One adventure leads to another, and each one has to be bigger than the last. You need a bigger hit. And sometimes the bigger hit just seems wrong."

I thought about the group meeting at the community centre.

"This time away has been like a detox," Glenn

went on. "I went through withdrawal and now I'm clean." He looked guilty. "I feel bad for saying these things. I feel bad for feeling them, especially given what he did for the team, what he did for me and the guys. Promise me you won't tell him what I said?"

"I won't. I kind of understand."

The gym door opened and the coach poked his head out. "Hey, get back in here now!" he yelled.

"I'd better get going. Later." He ran back into the gym and disappeared. Even through the closed doors I could hear the coach shouting at them.

I had to get going too.

I was relieved to see Ethan still parked in front of the school. But I was surprised to realize that I was also somehow a bit disappointed. If he hadn't been there, I could have just gone home, done some homework, maybe watched some TV. I could have eaten a meal with my parents and gone to bed early. Being with Ethan was always either exciting or amusing but, just as Glenn had said, it was also tiring. There were no dull moments, but there was no downtime either. I'd never thought of him as being a drug, or addictive, but Glenn was right.

Ethan was perched on the hood of his car. He was, as always, holding court, surrounded by a half a dozen guys, laughing, telling stories and jokes. Music was blaring out of the car speakers.

As I walked up, everyone turned and said hi. They knew me, but I certainly didn't know more than about half of them. It was funny, I'd been in the school for six weeks but Ethan was still the only person I hung around with, the only person that I'd have called a friend. And part of me was fine with that. I was only here this one year, and then I'd be gone to college. Besides, having friends didn't necessarily work out for the best, as I'd discovered.

"You ready to go?" Ethan asked me.

I nodded. He finished the last bit of his story and soon we were on our way.

"Are you up for something different today?" Ethan asked excitedly.

"I am, but could that something possibly involve a coffee first? I'm really, really tired."

"You do look a bit worn down," he said.

"I was up most of the night catching up on school. How do you do it? How come you're not dragging your butt around today too?"

"You already identified the solution. I hardly ever waste time on school-related matters."

"Aren't you planning on going to college next year?" I asked.

"I'm not worried. My father is not only an alumnus, he's a major contributor and connected to people on the board of governors of one of the best Ivy League schools. Unless I shoot somebody, I'm pretty well guaranteed admission."

"It must be nice."

"You'd think so, wouldn't you?" he said, and shook his head.

I waited for him to say more, but he just cranked the wheel and we squealed into the parking lot of a

small plaza. There was a little restaurant at the end
and he took a spot right in front of it.

"Looks a little tacky," I said.

"Places like this always have the best club sandwiches, coffee, and fries."

We headed in and sat down at a table by the window. A waitress came over and gave us two plastic-
coated menus.

"No need for menus," Ethan said. "We'd like two
coffees and two of your famous club sandwiches."

"You got it." She started away.

"Excuse me," Ethan called out, and she turned.
"What's your name?" he asked.

"Rita," she replied, with a big smile.

"Rita, that's one of my favourite names in the
world."

"Is it?" she asked.

I sat back and let him talk. Did he ever stop playing the game? The waitress was attractive but she had
to be in her early thirties.

"It's the name of my sister, who's named after our
great aunt. Someday it'll be the name of my daughter,
if I'm ever blessed enough to have one."

"That's so sweet."

"Do you know that Rita in Spanish means 'pearl,'
and in many other cultures it means 'perfection'?"
Ethan asked.

"I didn't know that," she said.

"I think there's something magical about names.
I've never met anybody named Rita who wasn't wonderful, who wasn't a pearl."

She looked even more pleased. "I'll be back with your coffees."

"How do you know what Rita means?" I asked him after she left.

"I know the meanings of over two hundred different girls' names."

"Sure."

"You doubt me? Go ahead and try me."

"Um . . . how about Anna?" I asked, using my mother's name.

"It was Greek, originally, and it means 'favour' or 'grace.' Do you want to keep testing me?"

"Go ahead, give me some more meanings you know."

"Would you like to know the meaning of Jennifer?" he asked.

There was that fork sticking into me again. Was it to taunt me, or was it just to show off?

"I don't need to know that one," I said.

"It's enlightening," he went on. "It's a version of the old Welsh name Guinevere, and it means 'fair one' or 'white enchantress.' Seems to apply, don't you think?"

"More than I'd like."

"And Raine, do you know what that means?" he asked.

"It means weather system?"

"No, it's from the French and it means 'queen.'"

"And Raine was one of the names you already knew?" I questioned.

"No, I looked that one up the night we met her."

"And you did that because . . .?" I asked.

"I just thought it might be useful. You know, for making conversation."

"So the real story is that you studied all this stuff about names to use when you meet girls. Knowing their name is part of picking them up."

He smiled. "Yes, young Grasshopper, you are learning. Did you notice how it impressed our pearl of a waitress?"

"Don't you ever turn it off, though?" I asked.

"It's the ten thousand hour rule."

"Another rule?"

"This one isn't even mine, but it's good. It states that if you want to get good at something, anything, you have to do it in a deliberate way for ten thousand hours to achieve mastery."

"So that's why you're trying to pick up the waitress?" I asked.

"Just practising. It comes naturally."

"She is, um, pretty, but isn't she a bit old?"

"You didn't strike me as an ageist."

"I try not to discriminate against anyone, least of all because of age," I retorted.

"That's good to know. I'm prepared to date anybody, regardless of race, religion, linguistic group, or age—assuming legal requirements are met."

"Okay, I understand, but, face it, she's old enough to be your mother."

"Not unless my mother was fourteen or fifteen when she had me."

The waitress reappeared with our coffees.

"Rita, could you answer a question for me?"

"Sure, honey."

"It's very personal."

"The more personal the better," she said. It was obvious from the lilt in her voice that she was flirting with him, too.

"My little brother here and I have a small bet, and whoever guesses closest gets his meal paid for by the other. Could you tell us how old you are?"

Now she looked taken aback.

"He thinks you could be twenty-four or twenty-five years old," Ethan said.

Or thirty-four or thirty-five, I thought, but didn't say.

"A little bit older," she said.

"That can't be. I had you at twenty-two, tops," Ethan said.

She giggled as though she was actually thirteen. "Well, I'll be twenty-six on my next birthday," she answered. She looked down, slightly, and blushed a little bit. She was either embarrassed or she was lying. I had my money on the latter.

"I'm assuming that your birthday is at least thirty-six months away. And since I lost the bet, could you make sure this lunch is on one bill and give it to me?" Ethan said.

"Maybe I should have ordered something more expensive than a club," I joked.

"Rita, I think you have the same problem as me," Ethan said.

"What's that?"

"People think I'm younger than I actually am. How old would you guess I am?"

"Twenty, maybe twenty-one?" she guessed.

He didn't look that old.

"I'm actually twenty-five myself."

"You do look younger," she said.

"It's this baby face. I do put it to good work, though. Other lawyers often underestimate me in court."

"You're a lawyer?"

"Yes. By the way, my name is Eugene, and this is my baby brother, Goose, short for Gooseberry."

Once again I had a truly stupid name.

"Gooseberry?" she asked.

"Our mother was a bit of a hippie. The strangest thing is that our last name is Bush, so my brother is actually Gooseberry Bush."

"Oh, that must be hard," she said.

"It's had its moments," I said, "although it's not nearly as embarrassing as Eugene's full name. He's actually Eugene Lynn Evelyn Bush."

Ethan looked genuinely pleased that I'd been able to come up with that. Instead of being embarrassed he seemed quite happy about it.

"What can I say, I was named after my mother's father and then both of our grandmothers," he said.

"It must have been a very hard labour—that's the only reason I can think of for it," I added.

"It was thirty-six hours of hard labour, breech birth, and I weighed almost eleven pounds. I apologize to my mother on a regular basis for putting her through that."

"Mom still talks about it when she's had a glass of wine or two at dinner," I added. Ethan had taught me that details always made a story much more believable.

"Do you like lawyers?" Ethan asked Rita, who had been laughing along at all these stories.

"More than dentists, I guess," she replied.

"That's a pretty low standard—everybody hates dentists," I said.

"Probably not their mothers, unless they went through more than thirty-six hours of hard labour. So, Rita, you'd be more likely to go out with a lawyer than you would a dentist, right?" he asked.

"I guess that depends on whether the lawyer was cute."

Ethan put a finger to his chin and turned it around like he was making a dimple. I had to stop myself from rolling my eyes. "I've been told that some people think I'm young-looking but reasonably cute. Tell you what, you don't have to say yes, but please don't say no . . . think about it."

"I'm thinking."

"I'm a delicate soul. Could you do me a favour? Say yes by adding in a few more fries to go with my club sandwich, and if the answer is no, give me the regular order and we'll all just pretend that I never asked you. Could you do that?"

"I could do that," she said.

Rita gave Ethan a big smile and then turned and walked away.

"Tell me you didn't do all that just so you could get extra fries," I said.

"The fries are simply a bonus. By the way, Lynn Evelyn, that was a very nice touch."

"Gooseberry Bush wasn't bad either."

"Well, brother Goose, I really do want to go out with her."

"You don't really believe she's twenty-five, do you?"

"No more than I believe that she thought I was twenty-five," Ethan said. "I figure she's about thirty-five, which means she's closer to my mother's age than mine."

"Then it *would* be like dating my mother."

"Um . . . I really like your mother and think that's she very attractive, so if your father wouldn't mind—"

"I think we'd all mind," I said.

"And if it eventually developed into more, I'd even let you call me E-Daddy—which is sort of a great name if I ever become a rapper."

"You've got a much better chance of becoming a rapper than dating my mother," I said.

"You never know."

"Oh, I do," I said, "because if my father didn't kill you, I'd do it myself."

"Threat taken and noted. By the way, have you ever dated an older woman?"

"In seventh grade, for a week, when she was in grade 8."

"I said woman, not girl. Women are different. Fewer games . . . at least on their part."

"You've dated women before?"

"The oldest was in her forties. Rita will be a lot of fun. Did you notice what I accomplished with her?"

"So far all I've seen is you trying to pick up an older woman. We'll have to wait until the fries arrive to decide if you accomplished anything," I said.

He shrugged. "Success is never guaranteed. It's about technique. I told her she looked younger than she is."

"So you flattered her."

"It's about the direction of the flattery. Older women want to be thought of as younger. Younger women want to be thought of as older. If I'd thought she was eighteen, I would have said she was twenty or twenty-one."

"Which is, come to think of it, what Rita did with you," I pointed out.

"You know we're not the only ones playing the game. It fits with all pieces of the puzzle. Smart females want to be seen as pretty and pretty ones want to be thought of as smart. It works on so many levels. You figure out what they aren't, which is usually what they want to be, and make them think that's how you see them."

"Do you have a name for this theory?" I asked.

"Of course. I call it Reverse Typology."

"Did you just make up that name?"

He smiled. "I did, and I'm very proud of it. Always call them the type that they aren't.

It's just another interesting part of the overall game theory."

"And you like the game," I said.

"I *love* the game."

"So for you this is no different than a spirited game of Dungeons and Dragons."

"Of course it's different! Dungeons and Dragons? That's for full-blown nerds. No, think of it as a classic, like Monopoly, where you try to win all the assets, or my new favourite, Settlers of Catan, where you're gathering resources. And speaking of resources, do you want me to see if Rita has a younger sister or friend for my baby brother?"

"Actually, I was going to talk to you about that."

"No worries, as soon as she brings me the extra fries I'll arrange for it."

"Thanks, but no thanks. That's not what I meant. What I'm really looking for is a little time out. I just can't go at it every night like you do. Is that okay?"

"Of course it's okay. This isn't a prison sentence. It's not like you're getting time off for bad behaviour. I know it's hard to maintain this pace," Ethan said. "I've been in training a long time. I am a serious professional athlete."

"Which makes me an amateur?"

"Don't be so hard on yourself. I think of you as a rookie with potential to be rookie of the year."

I bowed slightly from the waist. "I am honoured."

"You should be. Besides, I think you should save yourself for a field trip the two of us should go on. Is there anything special happening in the hick town where you grew up?"

"Well, eventually Christmas . . . wait, you want to go back to my hometown?"

"Of course not. I don't want to go there but you need to, and you won't be going alone. It'll be you and me, and the two most spectacular dates anybody in Hicksville could even imagine."

"Wow, that would be . . . amazing."

I pictured the whole scene. We'd walk into my school and visit with my buddies, who would be drooling over the girls. I'd be getting high-fived by them, all of them, including my old "friend" Elmer. *He* would be jealous. And the whole time *she'd* be standing next to him, but watching us. I'd glance at them, maybe give a little wave and a smile, but that's all. I'd act like I was so over it. Like the relationship, the ending, the betrayal all meant nothing to me. *I'd* have the last laugh. At least on the outside.

And then I thought about who I'd want to take back—Raine. I knew she wasn't who Ethan would think of, and probably not the sort who would blow away Elmer—unless he got talking to her.

"You have to admit that would feel really, really good," Ethan said, his words snapping me back to reality again.

"That doesn't even come close to describing it."

"So that's what we'll work at . . . after you take some time off. Anyway, I'm going to be occupied this week with Rita."

"Maybe you shouldn't count your fries until they're delivered."

Rita came up to the table with two plates. She placed a club sandwich with fries in front of me. The other plate she placed in front of Ethan. I could only assume that somewhere buried beneath all those fries piled high on his plate was a club sandwich.

Ethan picked up a fry, pointed it at me, and smiled.

CHAPTER THIRTEEN

Tuesday was quiet. I came straight home from school, had dinner with my parents and sister, did some reading for class, started an assignment that wasn't even due for another week, and then went to bed early.

Wednesday, Ethan didn't show up at school. Apparently he had told Rita that he'd skip "court" to spend the day with her. He texted a couple of pictures of Rita dressed casually without her waitress uniform—she was definitely worth looking at, no matter how old she was.

It had been a regular, solid, uneventful, rather boring day. Leaving school, I was almost disappointed not to have Ethan sitting outside, offering me not just a drive home but a drive to another adventure. It was okay, though. After all, it wasn't a Friday or Saturday. It was a good day to just head home and do a little homework—very little, since I'd managed to catch up on everything. Wednesday, the middle of week, was when nothing was supposed to happen. Of course, there was one thing happening, and I had been thinking about it all day—well, thinking about *her*.

The traffic on Lakeshore Avenue was buzzing along in all three lanes in each direction, at speeds that made me think the speed-limit signs were strictly for decoration. I moved along a walkway that was set back far enough from the road to give me a sense of safety and looked out toward the lake. The water was dark blue and extended to the horizon, making the lake look more like an inland sea. The wind was whipping up waves that were crashing up and over the breakwater, as well as pushing along a few small sailboats enjoying the wild ride. Those same winds swept away the vehicle exhaust fumes, so I could see and hear the cars but couldn't smell them. I missed the smell of the fresh air where I came from. People told me I'd get used to the city smell but it hadn't happened yet.

Then, up ahead, I saw them—a bunch of people standing on a concrete island as rivers of traffic flowed by them in both directions. Many of them held signs, and as I got closer, I could make out what some of them said: "Friends, Not Food," "Respect Life," "Witness." One had a picture of a pig and read, "We Deserve Empathy." Another had a picture of a dog and a pig and read, "Why Love One and Eat the

Other?" For a split second I thought they were endorsing eating dogs instead of saving pigs.

The protesters waved their signs at passing motorists. The cars were all moving so fast I had trouble believing they could even read them. Some honked their horns, but I couldn't tell if that was to express agreement or derision.

As I approached, one of the protesters turned around—it was Raine! I felt a rush of relief, and then instant anxiety. What did I do now? What was I supposed to say to her? Would she even remember me, or be glad to see me if she did? How embarrassing would it be if I had to introduce myself again? I thought about just turning around and leaving when she saw me. She smiled and waved, and I waved back.

As soon as the lights turned red, I crossed to the island. The protesters used the red light as an excuse to talk to the waiting drivers and passengers of the vehicles, or at least share the message on their signs. Some of the drivers grimly stared forward, trying their best to pretend nobody was there, while others gave thumbs-up or even rolled down their windows to talk.

"Dakota, it's good to see you!" Raine exclaimed.

"It's good to be here."

"I must admit this is a surprise. I didn't expect to see you or your friend again."

"But I said I'd like to come down here sometime," I said.

"People say lots of things. Do you want a sign? Sometimes it's good to let people see what you're thinking."

"Sure, why not."

She picked up a sign that was leaning against a post on the median and went to hand it to me. It read "Choose Vegan." Then she hesitated.

"This one is probably wrong. You're a vegetarian, not a vegan, right?"

I thought back to our conversation. "Vegetarian."

"That's what I thought. Those are leather shoes you're wearing, aren't they?"

I looked down at my feet. I was wearing a pair of leather dock shoes. "Yeah."

She leaned in closer and whispered, "It's probably better not to wear those here if you decide to come back. We occasionally have some pretty militant vegans who would object to you wearing the skin of a dead animal."

"Sorry, I wasn't thinking."

"It's okay. Funny how we're trying to extend empathy to animals but sometimes we forget to be kind to other people. If vegans and vegetarians can't get along, what hope does the world have?" she said, and laughed.

The traffic had already started up again, and the cars and trucks were zooming by, each one pushing aside the air to produce a little gust of wind.

"We're big on truth here," she said.

I had a rush of anxiety—had she found out about me?

"And that's why you can't have that vegan sign."

She put down the first sign and grabbed a second that read, "Friend, Not Food" and featured a very cute little piglet. I was grateful that she didn't know that this sign was no more applicable to me than the vegan one.

"While I have respect for their level of commitment, I do find vegans can be a little extreme about things," she said. "Although who am I to talk, when lots of people think we vegetarians are extreme. Are you a lacto-ovo-vegetarian?"

"Guess," I said.

"Um . . . that's tricky." She looked at me hard. "Yeah, I'd say you eat eggs and drink milk."

"Half right. I do drink milk."

I had also spent some time googling all this before I drove down, so I actually knew what this all meant. Another one of Ethan's rules involved doing your research.

"And you, do you eat eggs and dairy?" I asked.

She leaned in closer again. "Giving up meat was easy. Giving up a cold glass of milk with some cookies was impossible."

This time I leaned in. "How about if we keep that as our little secret?"

She looked pleased with that idea. I wondered if Ethan had a theory about bonding through shared secrets. I'd have to ask him.

Raine took me from person to person and introduced me. They were all very friendly and greeted me warmly, as if welcoming me to a little club. I was relieved that nobody commented on my shoes.

"Here comes a truck!" somebody yelled out, and everybody else turned to look down the road.

Driving along with its left-turn signal flashing was a large transport truck. Its brakes huffed and squealed as it slowed and then came into the turning lane beside us, gliding to a stop. Along the trailer's long metal side were several rows of holes, and instantly I could see movement through them. There were patches of pinkish skin pressed against some, and through others little snouts and ears were sticking out.

The protesters all reached out and pressed their hands against openings, talking to the pigs behind the steel. Some even poked their fingers through the holes, while others took pictures. There were three levels to the trailer, and those on the island could reach up only to the second. The third was almost beyond our sightlines, but I could still see little patches of pink sticking out.

Up front, one of the protesters was standing on the step of the truck. She reached up and handed the driver a bottle of water, which he took. They were talking, but I wasn't close enough to hear the words over the noise of the traffic.

I turned back toward the trailer and was startled to see an eye pressed against one of the holes directly in front of me, no more than two feet away, staring right at me. For an instant I thought it was a person, but of course it wasn't. It was a pig. The dark brown eye moved slightly, and then it blinked. It seemed to be studying me. I could only see the eye but it could observe all of me, all of the scene around me. In that eye I could see intelligence, trying to sort out the things it was seeing.

I thought I could see something else—uncertainty. No, it was more than that. I saw fear. And that bothered me more.

The truck shuddered and then slowly started forward. The eye was gone, lost in the movement, the angle wrong, and the rows of holes became nothing more than a blur as the truck picked up speed, made the turn, and chugged off down the side street.

"Are you all right?" Raine asked.

I turned to her. "Sure . . . good . . . okay . . . why?"

"You look a little bit off."

"Maybe it's being out here, all the traffic zooming by, the fumes from the cars. It's disorienting. Those trucks, how often does it happen, how often are they here?"

"Each day five thousand pigs pass through this slaughterhouse."

"That's a lot of pigs."

"Sometimes there are five or six trucks every hour. There'll be another along within ten minutes or so." She looked at me again, this time harder. "Are you sure you're okay?"

"Maybe I need to sit down. My legs are a little bit shaky."

CHAPTER FOURTEEN

I took a sip of water. It felt good. Sitting down felt good. Sitting with Raine felt really good.

"You've finally got your colour back," Raine said.

"Is that colour red, from embarrassment?" I asked.

"There's nothing to be embarrassed about."

"I had to come and sit down." I thought about the next part and decided to say it anyway, because it wasn't like it was a secret. "You know, I thought I was going to faint."

"Seeing it for the first time can be incredibly difficult and emotional."

"Almost more than I could handle."

"It affects caring people the most," she said.

Raine had taken me by the arm, walked me off the island, across traffic, and we'd sat down on the grass, close to the lake. We were so close that fine beads of water from the spray were occasionally hitting my face. I didn't mind. It felt good, and it seemed to help settle my stomach.

"It was looking at me," I said. "It was like it was a person, not an animal. I felt so, so . . . I don't know. I can't put it into words."

"It's hard to put a feeling into words, and sometimes it's not even possible or necessary. I understand."

"Thanks for saying that. I appreciate it. So . . . what happens after the trucks drive away?" I asked, although I obviously knew the answer.

"The gates of the slaughterhouse are down that road. It's just out of sight. But when the wind is blowing from that direction you can hear the pigs crying out."

"You can hear them?" I gasped. Thank goodness that the wind direction that day was off the lake.

"It's awful. Sometimes they cry out in pain, other times it's just because they are afraid, being pushed and shoved around by the handlers as they move them to the line where they're killed."

"I don't think I could ever eat bacon again," I blurted out, and instantly remembered I was supposed to be a vegetarian who didn't eat meat anyway.

"It's a good reinforcement for those of us trying to live the right way. It's a constant struggle."

"For you too?"

"It's not just that big glass of milk I crave. Sometimes when I wake up I'm thinking about eating a big, juicy burger," she said.

"With lettuce, onions, and mushrooms?" I added.

"Is that the way you used to like it?" she asked.

I nodded. I'd had one for lunch at school that day. I hoped it didn't still linger on my breath.

"At least I can still have the lettuce, onions, and mushrooms," I joked. "Nobody could object to that."

"You'd be surprised."

I gave her a questioning look.

"Some people believe that fruit and vegetables can also feel pain," she explained.

"You're joking, right?"

She shook her head. "There are people who will only eat fruit that has been *surrendered* by the tree."

"I have this image of apples and oranges with little hands raised in the air."

"The fruit has to fall from the tree before they harvest it," she explained.

I couldn't help but laugh, and then tried to hide it in case I was offending her.

"I know, it does sound a bit silly," she said.

"So if they want a carrot do they have to wait until the ground shoots it up into the air?"

She giggled. It was such a wonderful sound that I couldn't help but smile. "Okay, maybe a bit more than a little silly," she said.

"I guess we need to admire their commitment. It's better than eating bacon," I suggested.

"It is. If you're interested, there are videos taken inside the slaughterhouse that show the process," she said.

"That's probably the last thing I should look at right now."

"I think if people had to watch footage like that they'd never eat meat again," she added.

I shuddered, and my stomach did a little turn.

"Most of the time when we protest it feels like we're just preaching to the converted," Raine said. "The people on Pig Island are already committed. It's the people who are passing by we want to reach. If we could convert just one person, convince one person to think more about it, then that would mean so much. But I guess we'll never know if we do have an impact."

"You do, you do," I said. "I know your actions do have an impact on people." I just couldn't tell her I was the one who had already been changed. Could I ever look at a piece of bacon again without seeing that eye looking at me?

"I understand that some people think we're all a bunch of nuts, standing out here on the island waving signs," Raine said.

"At least you're not waiting for carrots to jump out of the ground."

She laughed, and people turned around to look.

"We don't usually laugh a lot out here," she explained. "I just wish that the people criticizing our actions could understand the interconnectedness. The cruel use and abuse of animals causes abuse of people. It's in the best interests of mankind to not use animals for food. There are almost one billion people in the world who are malnourished. To feed a vegetarian takes a third of the land and water it takes to feed a meat-eater. If we could all become vegetarians, there would be enough food for everybody. But you know that. You were saying basically the same thing to me over coffee the day we met."

"I've thought a lot about our conversation," I said.

"Me too. That's why I was happy you came today."

She looked as though she was blushing, and I wanted to keep a good thing going.

"How about if we take that lettuce, onions, and mushrooms and split a salad some time?" I asked.

"Are you asking me out on a date?"

"Vegetarians are allowed to date other animals, aren't they?" I joked.

She laughed. "It depends on the type of animal."

"I was thinking one who's smarter than a toddler, but apparently has a very weak stomach for some things. Would you consider dating that type of animal?"

"It's about the only type I would date. I'm free Friday."

"That would be wonderful!" And then I thought of Ethan. He'd already mentioned us going out on Friday night. "Do you think one of your friends, Emma or Rachel, might be interested in going out as well so we could double with my friend . . . Orion?" For a second I'd blanked on his name. Hopefully she hadn't noticed.

"You hesitated," she said.

She had noticed. What now?

"Was that because you wondered if one of my friends going out with him might not be a good idea?" she asked.

"I think I just blanked because I was thinking about where I want to take you."

That was a convincing lie. Now I had to turn things around. One of Ethan's rules: it's better to ask a question than be asked a question.

"Why would you ask me that? Do you think they won't go out with him?" I asked.

"I think they'd both be willing to go out with him. I'm just not sure it would be good for them." She hesitated. "Please don't take offence, but he did seem a little glib, a little slick."

"No offence taken. Sometimes he can come across that way," I agreed.

"And Emma and Rachel are a little bit naive."

"I know he can come across as slick, but I think it's all about him not feeling very confident in himself." As those words came out of my mouth I wondered if they were, in any way, believable.

"I guess I can see that," she said.

"Orion is a lot of fun. In fact, fun is pretty well guaranteed."

She didn't answer right away. "I'll talk to Emma first and see if she's free."

"Great, I'll talk to Orion. If worse comes to worst, you'll be stuck with just me."

I got up and offered a hand to help her to her feet. "I'm keeping you from what you should be doing. Let's get back to the island."

"Are you sure you want to do that?" she asked.

"Yes, actually, I am." I paused. "But stay close in case you have to catch me."

CHAPTER FIFTEEN

"I can't believe you arranged to go out with Veggie-girl tonight," Ethan said as we pulled away from my house. We were headed to a restaurant to meet Raine and Emma.

"Why wouldn't I want to go out with her tonight?" I asked.

"Well, she's probably worthy of a Wednesday, or even a Thursday, but she's not Friday or Saturday material."

"Seriously? Where do you get these rules from?"

"A lot of what I know comes from studies analyzing hard scientific data. By the way, did you know that 23.1 percent of statistics are lies?"

"I believe that 23.1 percent of what you say is just bull," I said.

"Here's a tip: when you use made-up statistics

to back up an argument, always make it an uneven number. Apparently, that works 67.7 percent of the time."

I couldn't help but laugh. He was amusing about 95.3 percent of the time.

"So you don't disagree with me dating her," I said, "you just think I missed by a night or two?"

"Yeah. But it's not all about you tonight," Ethan said. "Your scheme involves tying up *my* Friday night, and that represents a big, big sacrifice on my part."

"I thought I was doing you a favour. I know how hard it is for you to meet girls or get a date."

He snorted. "Yeah, fixing me up with one of these girls is some big favour. I don't remember which one was Emma and which was Rachel but I do remember that they were way, way, *way* below my usual standard. Either one of them was more like a Monday afternoon sort of date . . . no, even that's stretching it."

"Then think of it as a favour you're doing for me."

"I'm actually thinking about it more as your *debt*. Now you owe me even more than you did before, and I'll ask for repayment to begin almost immediately."

"How immediately?" I asked, with some trepidation.

"I made a little arrangement. When you told me about this at lunch on Thursday, I did a bit of extra planning. You need to think of tonight as a double-header: date A and date B, one early and one late."

"You've arranged another date for us tonight?"

"I couldn't let a Friday go to waste. Rita has a friend."

"As in Rita the waitress who's old enough to be your mother, whose friends are probably old enough to be my mother?"

"That's the one. But she said she'd find a younger friend for you, because you, my little brother Gooseberry, are only twenty-one years old."

"So that means whoever she gets will be around thirty years old and will pretend to be about twenty-two. And you accuse me of wasting a weekend night," I said.

He shrugged. "I wouldn't have arranged it if you hadn't already killed the first part of the night. Think about it as two wrongs trying to make one sort of right."

"I'll think about it any way you want as long as you're nice to Emma," I suggested.

"I'm always nice. That girl is going to think that she's died and gone to heaven. At the end of the night she'll want to bear my children."

"You don't need to go that far. Just make sure she's happy so Raine is happy."

"I will make Raine so happy she will shine . . . get it, rain and shine?"

"Turn here. The restaurant is down this street," I said.

He made the turn practically on two wheels, coming dangerously close to another vehicle waiting at the corner, and slowed down only slightly as we went down the road.

"Just how many accidents have you been in?" I asked.

"None today, but the night is still young."

"There's a spot right in front," I said.

He pulled in, came to a stop, and looked up at the restaurant. I waited for his reaction.

"The Clever Bunny?" he asked.

"Cute name, right?"

"They offer rabbit on the menu?"

"Uh, no. Think about what rabbits eat."

"You mean . . . lettuce, carrots, vegetarian food?"

I nodded.

"Why didn't you tell me we weren't going to be eating real food? We could have gone into a drive-through and had a burger first."

That actually would have been good.

"No, wait, you didn't tell me because you were afraid I might not go along with it."

I shrugged. "Maybe a little. Raine is a vegetarian, and I guess, for tonight at least, so am I."

"And we're eating here because you're trying to make the lie live, or because Veggie-girl chose this veggie place for the meal?"

"Can't it be both?"

"In future, make sure you pick the place for meals, or whatever activity is going to happen. Always."

"Another rule?"

"Of course it's another rule. It's the Home Field Advantage rule. I should be charging you for this wisdom."

"Home field only applies to sports," I said.

"It applies to all games, including the one we're playing tonight. It gives you control. Never give up control."

"I'll try to remember that. And yes, she did choose the vegetarian restaurant."

He shook his head slowly. "That debt you owe me just got much, much bigger."

The whole restaurant was decorated in soft, washed-out earth colours. Everything was made of wood and bamboo. There was incense burning and soft pan flute music playing in the background. The hostess was wearing sandals and socks and a flowing dress, and she led us to our table, a corner booth.

"Thank you, Skye," Ethan said. "I *love* your name."

Her small, satisfied smile grew wider.

"Your name suggests freedom, flight, non-conformity."

I tried to refrain from rolling my eyes. Once again, he was trying to pick up the waitress.

"Could you bring us water, please?" I asked, trying to head this off before it got any further.

She smiled and left.

I leaned in toward Ethan. "And could you leave the waitress alone and save the flirting for Emma, please?"

"I have enough to go around, and it's not like Emma's here to be upset. Do you think they're going to show?" he asked.

"Of course they are. Why would you even ask that?"

"Partly wishful thinking so we don't actually have to eat here, and partly because it happens all the time. I've been involved in a number of dates where people were stood up."

"That was you standing them up!" I exclaimed.

"Like I said, I've been *involved*. It's all part—"

"I know, I know. It's all part of the game," I said. "Don't you ever get tired of it?"

"Sometimes, but it's not like I invented it. I've just learned to play it for self-defence purposes."

That was surprising. Self-defence? I'd never heard him put it that way before. "And who are you defending yourself from?" I asked.

"I play the game in a feeble attempt to even the playing field a little," Ethan said.

"So far, from what I've seen, you seem to have it strongly tilted in your direction."

Just then I spotted Raine and Emma coming in the door.

"There they are!" I said. I got up and waved so they could see us.

Raine was dressed casually—flowing dress and flats. Emma was in a black dress and was tottering awkwardly on enormously tall heels. She was dressed to go to a dance club, not a laid-back vegetarian restaurant. Obviously she was pretty excited about this date.

"So good to see you both," I said. "Emma, you remember Orion, right?"

"Of course!" She sat down on the bench right beside him. Very close beside him.

I pulled out a chair for Raine and then wondered if I shouldn't have done that. Was that an anti-feminist thing to do?

"This looks like a great place. I'm assuming you've eaten here before," I said

"It's one of my favourites. It's hard to find good vegetarian food."

"You wouldn't think it was that hard to find the recipe for salad!" Ethan joked, and Emma laughed along.

"It's a little more challenging if you expect the food to be organic and you try to follow the Hundred-Mile rule," Raine said.

"I know organic but I don't know what that Hundred-Mile rule means," Ethan said. "And believe me, I *love* rules." He shot me a glance.

"It involves purchasing only ingredients that are produced locally," I said. "Depending on the geographic area, it's often sixty to a hundred miles."

"How do you know that?" Ethan asked.

"I was in the Social Justice Club at my old school."

"You were in the Social Justice Club?" Ethan said with a laugh.

"Three years," I answered.

"How, how . . . cute," he said.

"Raine is involved in our school's social justice program," Emma said.

"No surprise there. In fact, I would have been shocked if she wasn't. Still, what's the reason for this hundred-mile thing?" Ethan asked.

"Purchasing locally means the transportation costs are much lower and the pollution is much less, because the crops have a smaller footprint," I added.

"I know potatoes have eyes, and cabbages and lettuce come in heads, but I didn't realize any vegetable had a footprint," Ethan joked.

Again Emma laughed, but Raine only smiled a little. Maybe she was just trying to be friendly.

"As well, when you purchase locally you have an opportunity to inspect the farms to make sure they follow correct procedures for organic farming and don't use pesticides or employ unethical practices," Raine said.

"That's important, because some places pretend to be organic but they're not," I added.

"That's awful!" Ethan exclaimed. "Can you imagine that level of dishonesty, pretending to be something that you're not?" I could tell he was trying to catch my eye, but I ignored him. If he was trying to make me uncomfortable, it was working.

"It also means that people in our community are employed, which supports the local economy," I added.

"And by consuming local products—"

"And that can be food, furniture, any consumer goods," I said, before I realized I'd cut Raine off. "Sorry for interrupting you."

"I understand. It's hard not to get passionate about these things." She continued, "There's also the fact that locally grown or made products are more likely to be from a small or family-owned business instead of one of the big multinationals."

Ethan turned to Emma. "Do you get the feeling that we've just been given a university lecture by two professors from Granola U?"

She giggled. I think she would have giggled if he'd burped. If this was his idea of being nice, he was missing the mark by a lot . . . No, wait, I'd asked him to be nice to Emma—I should have remembered to mention Raine, as well.

"Did you get together before the meal and write up your lecture notes?" he asked.

"No need to compare notes when you're speaking from the heart," I said.

"That's touching," Ethan said sarcastically.

"I think it's sweet," Emma said, contradicting him—which surprised me. "You two really have so much in common."

I looked at Raine and she gave me a little smile. She really was beautiful. The gold in her blue eyes seemed to sparkle even more.

"It sounds like the owners of this restaurant are very committed," I said, trying to change the subject. I was beginning to regret making this a double date; worrying about what Ethan might say next was putting me on edge.

"They're wonderful people. They'll probably come over to say hello before the evening is over," Raine replied.

"I'm a little confused," Ethan said. "There are sliders on the menu." He turned it around and pointed at the item.

"It's soy-based. No meat," Raine explained.

"Did you ever notice that they often make vegetarian food to look or taste or sound like meat, but nobody ever tries to make meat look or taste like vegetables?"

"I imagine that's because meat is generally more appealing," Raine said.

Ethan looked surprised by her admission. "I thought meat was murder. You vegetarians say things like that, right? I've heard Dakota say that."

Why was he doing this?

"Yes, some vegetarians do say things like that." I turned to Raine. "He likes to give me a hard time." I turned back to Ethan. "But he's not going to be doing that any more tonight, right, my friend?"

He held up his hands as though surrendering.

"I eat meat," Emma said, adding support to, and fuel for, Ethan.

At that instant, Skye, our waitress, returned. She and Raine hugged each other like long-lost friends. Ethan looked amused by the whole thing, his expression saying, "What do you expect?"

At my suggestion Raine ordered for all of us. It seemed like the best way to avoid letting Ethan make fun of the menu.

"So, Dakota was telling me all about the pig protest," Ethan said.

I wondered where he was going with this. I hadn't told him much, and I certainly hadn't told him anything about me almost fainting.

"I was so happy that he joined in," Raine said.

"It won't be the last time," I said, "although it wasn't easy."

"It's not easy, but it is important. It's an intense experience to bear witness to the slaughter of such beautiful, intelligent creatures," Raine said.

"So, if they were ugly and dumb it would be easier and we could eat them?" Ethan asked.

"Of course not!" I said, jumping in before Raine could. I was used to Ethan being charming—what was going on with him tonight? Still, Raine's eyes flashed in anger. Somehow that made them even more beautiful.

"Just checking," Ethan went on, "because I've read that turkeys are about the stupidest thing on the planet, and they're incredibly ugly. I was hoping if that was the case then eating turkey would be all right."

"No turkeys either, but it does feel worse when the animal is intelligent, like a pig," I said.

"Pigs aren't actually that smart. It's a well-known fact that two out of three of them are really, really stupid."

"No, you are completely, utterly wrong," Raine snapped. "Every study ever done shows them to be highly intelligent."

"Smarter than dogs," I added.

"That's not setting the bar very high because, really, I've never heard of a dog running errands or doing somebody's taxes," Ethan said. "But still, I know my statistics are correct. Two out of three pigs are extremely stupid."

"So, tell us, Orion, why do you believe pigs are not intelligent?" Raine asked.

"I didn't say all pigs. Out of three pigs in a well-known study, two of them thought sticks and mud were as strong as brick. That's why a wolf was able to blow down their houses and eat them. I believe you are all familiar with that study, correct?"

"That's so funny!" Emma squealed, sounding, unfortunately, a bit like a little piggy on her way to market.

"That's a fable, not a study," I said, trying to suppress my irritation.

"Fable, story, or study, it's all just semantics. Wolves, by the way, are never vegetarians, although they do probably follow the hundred-mile diet. But getting back to the protests, when you're on that traffic island, are you trying to stop the trucks from entering the slaughterhouse?"

"We're there to bear witness," Raine said.

"And make other people aware. That's the reason for the signs," I added.

"If you're after awareness, you need to hire a spider who can weave a gigantic web saying 'SOME PIG' or maybe 'RADIANT,'" Ethan suggested.

"If we could find a spider named Charlotte, that might work," Emma added.

"'I want to breathe the beautiful air and lie in the beautiful sun,'" Ethan said.

"You can quote from *Charlotte's Web*?" I asked.

"It was one of my favourite books when I was a kid."

"It's still one of my favourites," Emma said. "'I don't want to die. I want to stay alive, right here in my comfortable manure pile with all my friends.'"

"Another impressive feature of my date," Ethan said, and Emma blushed noticeably.

"You mentioned your old school," Raine said, looking at me and changing the subject. She seemed less than charmed by Ethan. Just another thing I really liked about her. She was able to see through him. That also worried me. Could she see through me, too?

"Yeah, my family just moved here. I lived my whole life in a small town about fifteen hours from here, but my father was transferred for a promotion. My new school practically has a larger population than my old town."

"But it's filled with lots of cool people," Ethan said, pointing to himself.

"And one day maybe I'll meet some of them," I said.

This time Raine burst into laughter. She had an amazing laugh, and it made her eyes even brighter and more beautiful.

"I thought you two hadn't been friends very long," Raine said.

"Less than two months," I said.

"But it's not the quantity of the time, it's the quality," Ethan said.

"Raine and I met in first grade," Emma said.

"I met my old best friend in kindergarten," I said.

"How'd that work out?" Ethan asked.

I shot him a dirty look. "It could have ended better," I said.

The waitress came over with our order. Thank goodness. I let out a sigh.

CHAPTER SIXTEEN

I finished up the last smidgen of food on my plate—partly because the food was really good, but also because there wasn't nearly enough of it. Veggies were delicious, but not very filling, and our waitress had only refilled the basket of bread twice. The bread was made from some sort of ancient grains with sunflower seeds, and if I'd had another half a loaf I might have been satisfied.

Ethan had switched from being difficult to being the perfect dinner guest—the way I'd always seen him. He'd been friendly to the waitress, but not flirty. He'd been attentive to Emma and kind to Raine. There had been no more cracks about vegans or pigs. He'd even complimented the food—repeatedly—and when the owners had come over to the table he'd charmed them and promised he'd be coming back.

It had been a nice meal. Not just the food, but the company. Raine was smart and wasn't shy about expressing her opinions—I liked that, even when it was me she was disagreeing with. I liked *her*. And unless I was reading her completely wrong, she liked me.

"Is there anything more I can bring you?" Skye asked as she cleared the table.

"Just the bill," I said.

"It's already been paid."

"By who?" I asked.

The waitress pointed to Ethan.

"It was the least I could do. Raine and Emma, I hope you can forgive me for being a bit difficult in the beginning, especially after Raine chose such a wonderful restaurant."

"We could have split the bill," I suggested.

"No way, Dakota. I needed to thank you for including me in this double date. And Emma, well, thanks for agreeing to go out with me. It's been such a pleasure."

Emma looked so happy she was about to burst.

"It's been a wonderful night, and—" Ethan's phone buzzed. "I'm sorry, I should have had that turned off during dinner." He looked at his phone. "Oh, I have to take it, this is my father." He put the phone up to his ear. "Hey, Dad, can I call you back? I'm just having . . . Really? . . . That's awful!"

What had happened? How bad was it?

"I'll be there right away," he said. Ethan put down the phone.

"What's wrong?" Emma asked.

"It's my grandmother . . . she collapsed. They brought her to the hospital."

"That's so awful," Emma said.

He nodded. Were there tears starting in his eyes?

"Is she going to be all right?" Emma asked.

He shook his head. "I don't know. I have to go." He got to his feet, took a step, and hesitated. "Dakota, do you think that . . . no, I can't ask."

"Ask what?"

"It's just that I'm feeling a bit shaky." He did look like he was trembling a little. "I feel bad even asking, but do you think that you could take me . . . that you could drive . . .?"

"I can drive. I can go with you." I turned to Raine. "I really have to go."

"Of course, you *should* go."

I got up and went to his side. Raine and Emma got up as well.

"Please let us know how everything is when you know, when you have a chance," Emma said.

"I will," Ethan responded.

"I'll call as well," I said. "Thanks for under-standing."

Raine got to her feet and gave me a big hug.

"We have to get going," I told her.

We hurried out of the restaurant, and Ethan handed me the keys to his car.

I climbed in, made a quick adjustment to the seat and mirror, started the car, and backed out of the space.

"Where is the hospital?"

"Hospital? Why would you think we were going to a hospital?" he asked.

"Your grandmother isn't in a hospital?" I had a sudden thought, a terrible thought. "Wait . . . is this just a con?"

"I had to get us out of there somehow. You know, to get to our second date."

I'd enjoyed being with Raine so much that I'd actually forgotten we were halfway through a double-header. Date B was next.

"So . . . your grandmother isn't in the hospital?"

"I certainly hope not. The lady is as healthy as a horse and could probably take the two of us in fist-fight. She's pretty feisty."

"You really are unbelievable sometimes," I said.

"Sometimes? I think I'm unbelievable almost all the time. Wait, did I have you fooled as well?"

"Completely."

"And that's why you're mad?"

"I'm not mad."

"You're not happy. Look, I know you wanted to stay there, and I put our exit off as long as I could. But I know you well enough to know that you wouldn't want to stand up our second dates. Right? That would be rude and inconsiderate to them."

"And you never want to be inconsiderate," I said sarcastically.

"Look, can we talk about this while we drive? Our dates are waiting. Besides, you should drive away so our first dates don't look through the window and see us sitting out here in the parking lot."

That gave me motivation. I started driving again. "I can't believe you had somebody call you."

"I called myself." He held up his phone and it rang. "I just have to push this button and it rings. Then I answered it and had a conversation with myself. I was pretty convincing, don't you think?"

"Very. So, let me guess, you didn't tell me what you were going to do because you wanted my reaction to be real," I said.

"That is correct, and it was. Raine also got to see how caring you are, being willing to end a date to help a friend. Not that you needed to, but you actually scored extra points with her for leaving. How's that for irony?"

"Thanks for the help."

"Turn left at the next intersection," Ethan said. "Besides, I did hang in there longer than I wanted to because I know you like Veggie-girl."

"I do like *Raine*," I said, emphasizing her name. "It would be nice if you called her by her real name."

"You might want to think about that choice. Do you know what *Charlotte's Web* taught me? I learned that you never name something you might have to slaughter. Giving Wilbur a name made it much harder in the end."

"I'm not planning on slaughtering Raine."

"Again with the semantics. Perhaps 'sacrifice' would be better. I know that you like her. It shows. And she likes you, too."

That made me feel better. "I think she does," I said.

"There's no question. She's giving off so many signals you'd have to be a fool to miss them. The problem, though, is that you like her more than she likes you."

I turned slightly to look at him. "Really?"

"Really. You know I'm pretty good at reading these things. And that's the danger. You have to remember that it has nothing to do with you. She has that basic vegetarian problem."

I waited for him to finish his thought.

"Vegetarians are so busy loving animals that they forget we humans are part of the animal kingdom too. A heart is only so big, and if the heart is completely occupied loving pigs there might not be room for people. In fact, on some sort of subconscious level there might be anger toward humans because they're the source of the inhumanity toward animals. I know I'm rambling a little, but doesn't that make sense?" Ethan asked.

"It does, in a strange, Ethan sort of way. I'm just surprised that you don't have a rule named for this," I said.

"How about the I Love All Animals Except People theory?" he asked.

I couldn't help but laugh.

"It's good to see you laugh, buddy. Don't get me wrong, I know you want to see her again, and that's why I didn't arrange to skip out early or stick them with the bill—out of respect for you. You can thank me later. Actually, after this next date is over you'll be thanking me again and again. Quick, pull in here!"

I slammed on the brakes, spun the wheel sharply, and turned into a mall.

"Nice driving."

"This coming from you?"

"I am a skilled, don't-try-this-at-home sort of driver. You squealed the tires accidentally. You do have a driver's licence, right?"

"That and a licence to kill, like James Bond."

"Driving like that could kill us. Now pull in there . . . go to the drive-through window. I didn't get nearly enough food at dinner and I have a craving for a burger. A double, topped with cheese and bacon. Doesn't that sound good?"

It did.

"Should we order two?" he asked. "I'll pay."

I didn't answer right away.

"Come on, you know you want it. She'll never find out, and it's not like you're really a vegetarian. We can even ask them to hold the bacon from yours and double it up on mine."

I pulled up to the speaker.

"Welcome to Burger King, can I help you?"

"Can we have a Whopper with bacon and cheese, and a second Whopper, hold the bacon." I turned to Ethan. "And this one's on me."

CHAPTER SEVENTEEN

I was soaked to the bone. Between the rain and the spray and splashes from the cars everything was soaked—our signs, our clothes, our shoes. None of the drivers were rolling down their windows to talk to us, and one by one the other protesters had packed it in. There were only a few of us left. I'd been glancing at my watch when Raine wasn't looking. We'd agreed to leave at 3:00, and that meant we had less than thirty minutes left.

I'd called her when I got up that morning to see if she wanted to go out for a coffee. The first thing she'd asked was 'how was Ethan's grandmother.' I told her she was doing 'fine.' I felt bad about lying to her but what choice did I have? She said she was going down to Pig Island and asked if I wanted to come along. That made me happy and a little nervous as well. I wasn't sure how my head and stomach would react.

I was feeling a little dragged out. It had been a late night. Ethan and I had met our second dates at a pool hall, one of those upscale places, not some grimy dive. We'd shown up a bit late but they were cool with that.

At first I'd felt more like a prisoner than a willing participant, but I did start to have fun. With Ethan, fun was the only option, and Rita and her "younger" friend were pretty cool. Not only were they better players than either of us, but they were hilarious, and playful. I ended up having a good time. Only that made me feel guilty, as if I were cheating on Raine.

The rain seemed to be getting stronger. Appropriately, Raine hadn't seemed to mind the weather. She was always smiling, offering words of encouragement to me and the others, waving her sign, and trying her best to talk to the drivers of the trucks as well as the other cars stopped at the lights.

It had been a very busy morning for the trucks. Between three and seven of them had rolled by every hour. A few of the trucks had been lucky enough to time it so that they could roll through the light and didn't need to stop in front of us. Most, though, had to come to a stop to wait for the light to change. For the pigs inside it didn't matter if it was sunny or rainy. They were being trucked to their deaths. Little ears and snouts stuck out through the openings, eyes peering out, trying to hear or smell or see what was going on. How terrifying it must be for them.

Somehow it seemed more fitting that it was raining. Funerals should always take place in the rain.

"Here comes another truck!" one of the remaining protesters called out.

I had been hoping that there wouldn't be any more. I just wanted to call it quits, to go and get dry. Raine had already agreed to go with me to have that cup of coffee, and that thought warmed me as much as the coffee itself was going to.

The truck glided and splashed up water as it pulled in. Didn't matter—there was no way we could get any wetter. Two women came forward to touch the pigs through the small openings. I didn't have it in me any more. I'd seen enough animals on their way to die for one day.

Raine went to the cab of the truck, reached up, and offered the driver a bottle of water. The door flew open and a man jumped to the ground, holding a baseball bat.

"Get away from my truck!" he yelled.

Raine stumbled backwards, almost tumbling onto the road. For a second I stood stone-still, too stunned to even react.

"Go on, get away!" he yelled, slamming the bat against the side of the trailer.

One of the women screamed as the pigs inside squealed, and at that moment I became unfrozen. I jumped forward, positioning myself between the driver and Raine.

"What do you think you're doing?" I yelled.

"You people think you can do whatever you want!" he shot back.

"We're allowed to be here, we're allowed to protest peacefully!" Raine called out. She'd recovered
enough to talk.

"You're damaging my truck!"

"The only one who damaged it was you!" I said.
"Why don't you get back in the truck and drive away?"

"You can't tell me what to do!" he barked in reply.

He took a couple of steps toward me. I should have
backed away—I should have run away. I didn't. I stood
my ground and stared at him. He stopped a few paces
in front of me, just outside of swinging distance.

"Get back in your truck or we're calling the
police," I said. "Go. Now!"

He hesitated for a few seconds, then turned and
climbed back in the rig. The light had already changed
to green and his gears were grinding as the truck
bumped forward into the intersection. There was a
slight gap in the traffic and he started his turn in front
of oncoming vehicles. Drivers had to hit their horns
and slow down to avoid slamming into the side of him.

"Is everybody all right?" I asked.

"It's my turn to be a little shaky," Raine said.

"You're not the only one," one of the women said.

"I think we should call it a day," the second woman
said. "And Dakota, thanks for stepping forward."

"It was nothing."

"It *was* something," Raine said. "Thank you."

The coffee shop was little and funky, and as she had
at the vegetarian restaurant, Raine knew the owners

there. The coffee was, of course, organic, fair-trade coffee, and most of the treats were gluten-free. World music was playing overhead, and there was a large chalkboard where all sorts of sayings and bumper-sticker wisdom was written.

I glanced at my watch. "Wow, we've been here for over two hours."

"Really? I had no idea."

"You know what they say, time flies when you're having fun."

"I think I'll take that as a compliment," she said.

"You thought I meant spending time with you? I meant drinking coffee."

She looked surprised, and then amused. She reached over and gave me a little poke in the arm.

"Hey, no violence to animals, okay?"

She held up both hands in mock surrender.

"Okay, I'll admit that the person I'm drinking coffee with has something to do with the time passing so quickly."

She blushed. That was so sweet and wonderful and unexpected.

We went back to talking. Raine continued to tell me about her family, and while I listened I kept adding to the mental list of things I liked about her.

Her smile was big, and came easily and often, and made me want to smile. Her laughter was light and easy and almost musical, and it made me happy just to hear it. She had such blue, blue eyes, and, even better, those eyes belonged to a person who was intelligent, kind, defiant, opinionated, questioning, and caring.

She didn't wear much makeup because she didn't need to. Her hair, brown and long with a slight curl, was shiny, and I had this vision of her washing it only in rainwater—which today she had. My mother would have said she was a "natural beauty." Up to that point in my life, I hadn't really known what that even meant.

"Do you think Orion will see Emma again?" she asked.

I hadn't seen that coming, and I didn't know how to respond, so I just shrugged.

"She really likes him."

The polite response would probably have been, "And he likes her, too"—but that wasn't right. I settled for one true statement and a lie. "He's hard to predict. He doesn't really date much."

"Doesn't date much, or doesn't date the same person much?"

"Both . . . but mainly the last part."

"You know, I don't usually date at all," she said.

"Oh, you thought these things we were on were dates?" I asked. "These are simply two random instances of people who have common interests spending time together. Although, if you asked very nicely, we could be two friends who kiss."

She laughed. "Dakota, I really do like you."

There were two things wrong with that—Dakota wasn't my real name, and I was waiting for the "but" that was likely to follow.

"But . . ."

There it was.

"It's just that with school and all the different causes I'm involved with, and, college looming, I don't think I have any time left over for dating."

"Coffee isn't that much time. We could even drink instant coffee if that would help."

She laughed again. Was it a pity laugh? Did I sound desperate?

"You do make me laugh," she said.

"And you make me smile." I said it without thinking. It sounded so stupid, so glib, so much like a line, but it wasn't, because it came straight from the heart. "But I understand. No big commitments. Like I said, we're just a couple of people with common interests going out to do a couple of things, occasionally. Would that work?"

"I guess that could work."

"Good, because the alternatives seem to be that we either stop seeing each other completely, or we have to get married so we'll no longer be dating. And, quite frankly, I think we're a little young for marriage."

"Another thing we have in common. I really do feel comfortable with you. It's like we're not playing any games," she said.

I suppressed the urge to shudder in response. This whole relationship was based on an elaborate game that I was playing.

"Honesty is so important to me," she continued.

For a second I had this terrible thought that she knew everything and she was just taunting me. Maybe she was waiting for me to make a confession, and if I did it right now she'd forgive me and—

"I'd better get going," she said.

"Of course. I understand."

We got up and left the coffee shop, stopping under the canopy. Although it didn't seem possible, it was now raining even harder than before.

"I thought there wasn't any water left up in the sky," I said, holding my hand out to catch the rain. "I wish I had a car to drive you home so you wouldn't have to go out in this again."

"I'm not going to melt."

"I'll give you a call," I said.

"You'd better."

I wasn't sure what to do next. Was I supposed to kiss her, give her a hearty handshake, or . . .

She wrapped her arms around me and gave me a hug. Awkwardly I hugged her back. It felt like a hug reserved for your aunt. I couldn't be certain, but I got the feeling she was as confused as I was.

She released her grip and, without saying a word, turned and walked away. Was I an idiot for not trying to kiss her, or a bigger idiot for wanting to so much? Ethan was right. I did like her more than she liked me. That was so obvious, and potentially so painful.

She suddenly spun around and came walking back with a serious look on her face. Was she going to tell me that we couldn't see each other again?

She stopped, reached up, and kissed me. I kissed her back.

"Like I said, I don't date much, so I don't know how to do any of this stuff," she said.

"You did that part really well," I said.

She smiled, turned, and walked away into the rain again.

I stood there watching. I did like her, and she liked me back. I could only hope that she'd been making a mental list of things she liked about me, too. But then my stomach dropped. Me? Who was *me*? She only knew Dakota.

CHAPTER EIGHTEEN

After an afternoon spent trying to push thoughts of Raine out of my head so I could focus on a writing assignment for English—and failing miserably—Ethan called to fill me in on our plans for the evening. My heart sank, but I felt I owed him too much to say I'd rather stay in on a Saturday night. And now here I was, out at yet another club, with Ethan and two girls he had met while he was out getting groceries. He was like a wizard at this stuff.

"I've got to go to the washroom," Ethan's date said.

"I'll go with you," her friend offered.

"We'll be waiting right here," Ethan sang out.

We got up to allow them to slide out of the booth and they quickly vanished into the sea of bodies, swallowed up by the darkness of the club and the pulsing of the music.

Ethan sat back down right beside me. "What's with you tonight?"

"What do you mean?"

"You've hardly talked, and you keep missing what's being said. Do you even know their names?"

"Sure. Veronica is yours, and I'm with, um, Kristen."

"It's Kirsten, not Kristen."

"Sorry, it's really loud in here. But what does it matter? It's not like I'm going to end up with her anyway."

"It matters until we switch girls, or the switch won't matter," Ethan said.

Ethan had suggested that tonight we each focus on one girl and then, all of a sudden, out of nowhere, we change our focus to the other girl. He called it the Old Switcheroo manoeuvre. He said it would throw off their confidence, confuse them, and change the game dynamics. I had no doubt he was right. But I was too tired to play the game. I didn't want to play any games. I didn't even want to be there.

My thoughts kept drifting back to Raine. Not just to the kiss, but to the guy with the baseball bat on Pig Island, the trucks and what all of that meant, the conversations we'd had about so many life and world issues, and, perhaps most important, what any of this could mean when she didn't even know my real name.

"Hey!" Ethan snapped his fingers in my face. "You drifted out again!"

"Sorry, I'm tired. I was up early today."

"You're really taking all the wrong courses," he said. "Physics, calculus, and advanced English are way too demanding. You have to stop wasting your time on school."

"I don't have a guaranteed college admission, so I have to work, remember?" I hadn't told him that I'd been to Pig Island again, that I'd taken Raine out for a coffee afterwards, or that we'd kissed. I didn't need to tell him any of those things to know what he'd say. Let him keep thinking I was tired because of school.

"You know, it's way too loud in here to talk or listen," I yelled over the music.

"If they haven't climbed out the window in the women's washroom, we can go someplace else. If we do, will you promise to get your head back into the game?" he asked.

"I'll try."

"'Try not. Do or do not. There is no try.'"

"You're quoting Yoda to me?"

"It seemed appropriate, young Luke."

Luke was the name he'd given me for the night. I'd expected a fake name that started with the letter G but I'd learned that, with Ethan, nothing was completely predictable. In retaliation I'd given him the name Kirk. If I was from *Star Wars*, then he was the captain of the *Enterprise* from the original *Star Trek*. He knew I didn't like *Star Wars* and I knew he didn't like *Star Trek*.

"Look, buddy, you know these two don't mean anything," Ethan said. "If you don't like them, we can be the ones to climb out the window in the men's washroom and we can find a couple of girls who are better. It's up to you." He stared at me. "Well, are you—are *we*—in or out?"

I thought for a few seconds. I knew he was willing to walk away if that's what I wanted. He really was a good friend.

"I believe I am now beginning to feel the force," I said.

"That's my boy!" Ethan yelled. "May the force be with you!"

"May the force be with us," I yelled back.

Ethan jumped to his feet, whooped, gave me a double high-five, and then started twirling an imaginary lightsaber. He was still at it when the two girls returned to the table. They looked amused and a bit confused—not nearly as confused as they were going to be, though.

I was fighting to keep my eyes open. I was incredibly tired, but Ethan was drunk, so I was the one behind the wheel. I'd park him and his car at his place and walk home from there. We were almost there.

Ethan drinking had surprised me. He liked to be in control—correction, he *loved* to be in control—and the alcohol had taken that away. Our dates with Veronica and Kirsten had relocated to their apartment, but it had all ended in a less than stellar way, with Ethan drinking their alcohol, vomiting on their carpet, saying some negative things about both of them, and us finally being asked to leave.

On the drive home, he'd made a number of comments about how life "sucked" and he was "tired of all the games," and he'd mumbled something about some girl whose name got lost in a coughing fit. Then he'd passed out.

It had been a long night. Veronica, the one I'd ended up with after the switch, had spent a lot of time talking about her "fave" TV programs, which were all reality shows, and her hair, which she seemed to like *tremendously*. Perhaps she was hoping that her hair would get its own reality TV show. She'd taken a whole lot of pictures—including what seemed like dozens of selfies—and tweeted a steady stream all evening. She was so busy reporting on the evening that it was almost like she was only there as a visitor.

In hindsight, it wasn't that she was bad or wrong or shallow so much as that she just wasn't Raine. If Ethan's Theory of Relativity worked with physical appearance, it had to work with other things as well. Raine had so much to say about so many things that didn't have to do with reality TV shows.

I turned off the headlights before driving into Ethan's driveway to make our arrival less conspicuous. Then I remembered that he'd said his father was probably going to be out all night himself. Apparently, we weren't the only ones "out on a date." I had to wonder how weird it would be to have a father who was dating. My father would be home, long ago in bed, beside my mother, after watching *SNL* and having a bedtime snack of chocolate ice cream and a piece of toast. His routines—like the man himself—were predictable and sure and safe.

I liked my father. I liked my mother. And, more important, they liked each other. It wasn't that they didn't argue or fight or bicker, but they were good at making up, and they never seemed to stay mad at each other. Sure, there were some awkward, embarrassing, want-to-die moments when I'd stumble into the kitchen and they'd be kissing, but really, how wonderful was that? Wasn't that what everybody wanted . . . even Ethan?

I pulled the car up as close as possible to the front door, in case I couldn't get him on his own feet and I had to carry him. I circled around to the passenger's side and opened his door. He was slumped in the seat, all kinked up, gently snoring.

"Ethan, time to get up," I said, giving him a little shake.

One eye opened, and then the other. "What if I don't want to get up?"

"Then you can sleep in your car."

"House is better. Bed is better."

He needed my help to get out of the car.

"Which of these opens the door?" I asked, holding up his keys.

"Key pad by the door . . . 0703," he said. "It's my birthday . . . isn't that special?"

I punched in the code. The pad beeped and the door clicked. I led him inside.

"Okay, you're home. I'm going to leave your keys by the door."

"How will you get home?" he asked.

"I can walk. It's not far."

"Take the keys; take the car. You have to. I don't want you to walk. You know, you're a good friend."

"You're a good friend too."

"I don't have many friends," he said.

"Are you kidding? You have more friends than anybody I know."

He shook his head. "Shallow serial socialization is my specialty."

"What?"

"I know lots of people and lots of people know me. I don't really know any of them and none of them really know me. It's just that . . . I think I have to vomit again. Go home; take my car."

I was going to argue when he stumbled away and into a little restroom just off the foyer. I could hear the sound of him retching.

I held the keys in my hands. It would be faster to drive. I'd bring his car back in the morning.

CHAPTER NINETEEN

Sunday morning I dragged myself out of bed. I had to return Ethan's car, and I had a school assignment due on Monday. But first things first—I needed to eat something.

Before I was even down the stairs I could hear voices and laughter coming from the kitchen. Also wafting up the stairs was the aroma of bacon. It smelled so good . . . but it felt so wrong even thinking that. I wasn't a vegetarian, but I was starting to wonder if I'd ever eat anything that came from a pig again. Would I ever be able to smell bacon again without seeing that eye looking back at me? Might this bacon even be from that pig? I shuddered at the thought.

"Good morning," I said as I walked in.

"Morning, big guy," my father said. He was standing at the stove, making breakfast.

My mother was reading the paper. I stopped and gave her a kiss on the top of her head.

"That's very sweet," she said. "What did I do to deserve that?"

"He probably wants something," Olivia chipped in from across the table.

"I wanted to let our mother know how wonderful she is and how much I appreciate her."

"Even sweeter," she said.

"Personally," my father said, "I hope you do want something . . . breakfast?"

"Yes, please . . . well, some pancakes. I'll pass on the bacon."

"But that's the best part!" he said, and then he hesitated. "I guess I understand."

I'd told my parents about being at Pig Island and what went on there.

"You don't mind me cooking bacon, though, do you?" my father asked.

"No, of course not . . . not really . . . no."

"That's a relief. I love bacon. I'll have your share."

I sat down at the table and my father brought over a plate piled high with a stack of pancakes and a couple of pieces of toast. It smelled good. Not as good as the bacon, but good.

"I really didn't expect you to be up so early," my father said.

"It's not *that* early," my sister said.

"It is when you get home as late as your brother did," my mother answered.

"I tried to be quiet. I didn't wake you up, did I?"

"Of course not," she said.

"But that's only because your mother has trouble getting to sleep until you do get home," my father explained.

"Then I'm really sorry I was that late."

"Maybe you should give him an earlier curfew," Olivia suggested.

"I don't have a curfew," I said as I stuffed my face with pancakes.

"That's not fair!" Olivia protested.

"Your brother is almost eighteen and heading off to college next year," my mother said.

"And we completely trust him to do the right thing," my father said.

I consciously worked not to look away. What would they think about me if they knew the sort of games Ethan and I were playing with people?

"I want to talk to you all about something," I said.

"This sounds ominous," my father said.

"It's not. You know how we're getting a new dog in the spring? Well, I'm going away next year, so I thought Olivia should have my vote as well as hers in deciding on a name," I said.

"Really?" Olivia exclaimed.

"You're my baby sister and I know you'll choose a good name because you have such good taste."

"You're not going to kiss me on the top of my head too, are you?" she asked.

"Not unless you want me to. So, what names are you thinking about?" I asked.

"I'm not sure. I *was* going to suggest Jazz or Shadow, but now I have another idea."

"What is it?" my mother asked.

"I was thinking Raine."

I heard my father try to stifle a laugh.

I tried not to miss a beat. "That's a nice name," I said.

"I thought you might like it," she said.

"So, are you ever going to tell us more about the mysterious Raine?" my father said.

"And when are you going to invite her over?" my mother asked.

I shrugged. How could I ever bring her here to meet them?

"No pressure," my father said. "Well, not much."

"I'm not sure what there is to tell that I haven't told you already," I said.

"You haven't told us much of anything," my father replied.

"She's in grade twelve. She thinks she might want to be a doctor. She's big into social justice issues. She's a vegetarian. She's got blue eyes, and she's tall. She's not into trends or social media. She's not even on Facebook."

"I love Facebook," Olivia said.

"Yeah, we know," I replied.

"Just because you don't like it doesn't mean it's not good. You learn all sorts of things from looking at Facebook," she said.

"Such as?"

She looked as though she was going to answer, but then she stopped.

"Can't think of even one thing?" I taunted.

"I know that Jennifer isn't dating Elmer any more," she blurted out.

"What?"

"They both changed their status to single last week."

I wanted to laugh, but that wouldn't have been nice. But then, something different overcame me.

"That's too bad . . . for both of them."

"I thought you'd be happy," Olivia said.

"Why would I be happy that one of them, or maybe both of them, got hurt?"

"If it was me, then I'd want them both to get hurt," Olivia said.

I shrugged. "Maybe I did want that to happen, you know, before. But now I just feel sorry for both of them."

"That's very kind of you," my father said.

"Maybe I've just moved past all of that."

"Now I really need to meet this Raine girl," my mother said.

"Yeah, me too," my father agreed. "I'm assuming she's a part of this moving on."

Ethan had said the best cure for one girl was a better girl. I didn't imagine my parents were thinking about it the same way.

"Just be careful," my mother said.

"Relationships are tricky, but it's all worth it when you find the right person." My father went over and gave my mother a little peck on the cheek, and she giggled. It made me smile as well. Olivia, on the other hand, was making pretend gagging noises.

"You two really do like each other, don't you?" I asked.

"She's okay," my father said.

"Yeah, I kind of like him . . . you know, most of the time."

"Seriously, I'm asking," I said.

She nodded. "I love your father, but I like him just as much as I love him." My mother looked over at my dad as she spoke.

And my dad quickly jumped in with, "She's my best friend. I trust her with my life . . . although not necessarily with my car keys."

"Are you ever going to let me forget that I lost them?" she asked.

"Lost them twice," he said under his breath.

"I heard that. Technically, we found the second set of keys."

"Two months later, in the freezer," my father retorted. They were both laughing now.

"So, are you hitting the books today?" my mother asked.

"I will, but first I'm going to go out for a run." And of course I had to return Ethan's car—which they didn't even know I had. I'd parked it down the street.

"Do you want some company?" my father asked.

"Well . . . I was sort of hoping to go on my own . . . you know . . . I want to go faster and farther."

"Oh, I get it. I'm old and slow. Never mind. I understand."

"Sorry, old guy!" I gave him a pat on the head as I left to change my clothes.

—

I left the house, telling my parents I was off for my run, but instead I started jogging to where I'd parked Ethan's car. I'd almost pulled into my driveway last night before I'd realized how much I did not want to explain to them why I'd driven home in my friend's $85,000 BMW convertible at 4:00 a.m. Thank God it was still there, waiting for me. I climbed in and started it up. The engine purred like a big, contented cat.

I put on my turn signal and carefully checked the rear-view and side-view mirrors before I pulled away. No matter how much I liked it, I was a little nervous driving a car that expensive, and I just wanted to get it safely back in Ethan's driveway. I'd drop it off and then run back home so that my story about going out for a run wouldn't be a complete lie. I wasn't happy that lying was starting to come so easily to me.

Being up early meant I would have time to actually get ahead in my school work. Maybe I'd text Raine, see if she was free, and—no, that was the last thing I should do. I needed to play it cool. I wasn't going to be a hammer, but I certainly didn't want to become a nail.

I'd started to make a new list: things that Raine thought she knew about me that she didn't. Little things, like where I lived in the city. Bigger things, like the fact that I wasn't actually a vegetarian. Biggest things, like the fact that my name wasn't really Dakota. That list was really starting to weigh on me.

I eased into Ethan's driveway. There were no other cars. Either his father still wasn't home or his vehicle was tucked away in the garage. If Ethan had the BMW convertible, I was curious to know what kind of car his dad drove—it must have been something amazing. Now that I was there, I wasn't quite sure what to do with the keys. Then I caught sight of the keypad by the front door. After punching in the code, which I had miraculously remembered, I opened the door a bit and peeked in.

"Hello?" I called out quietly.

There was no answer. The foyer was empty but brightly lit. I'd just drop the keys on the side table and text Ethan later to tell him where they were. I stepped inside and—

"And who would you be?"

I jumped and looked around for the voice. A man wearing a suit and dress shirt but no tie was standing on the stairs, looking down at me. Ethan's father, I presumed. Either he'd gotten up early and was dressing for a meeting or he'd just got home from his date.

"I'm Graham, one of Ethan's friends. I was just dropping off his car." I held up the keys as some form of proof.

"Why would you have my son's car to begin with?"

"He asked me to drive. He wasn't feeling, um, well last night."

"Alcohol can do that to a person. I'm afraid he has his mother's tolerance level. What did you say your name was?"

"Graham, sir."

"Sir? Is that insincerity or politeness?"

"Politeness. My parents have never been good with insincerity but they're really big on manners."

THE ART OF PICKING UP GIRLS

"Well, polite Graham, would you like to join me for a coffee?"

He was tall and tanned and had that look of money that Ethan talked about. And there was something in his words, in his manner, that was so much like his son. But he reminded me even more of a game show host, or some actor whose name I couldn't remember.

He smiled. "It's not every day that I get to meet one of my son's friend. Please, join me. Berta has put out a breakfast spread. Do you like omelettes?"

"I'm not into eggs . . . or bacon."

"Are you a vegetarian?"

That was the first time somebody asked me that question when I could answer with some honesty. "I'm sort of trying."

"I'm sure Berta can find you something else. Please, join me."

I felt I didn't really have much choice. Maybe I could drink a coffee quickly and get back to finish up my school work.

"This might be the best coffee I've ever had," I said.

"Thank you," Berta said as she refilled my cup. "It's nice to see you again."

"It's nice to be back."

"Berta is a treasure who keeps our lives moving forward," Mr. Frost said.

"Perhaps if I'm that valuable you should consider paying me more," Berta replied.

"You're not happy with your wages?"

"I could always be happier."

The coffee had led into a full-fledged second breakfast for me, with fruit, pancakes and maple syrup, and freshly baked muffins with homemade jam. And for my second breakfast once again I'd turned down the bacon, and this time some sausages as well.

"Actually, all the food is amazing. If I were you, Mr. Frost, I'd try to make sure Berta was really, really happy," I said.

"Hey, whose side are you on?" he asked.

"I'm on the side of the person who made this feast!"

"Before you break open my bank for Berta, you should know that this spread is only offered on Sundays."

"You make it sound as if I don't feed you the rest of the time!" Berta scoffed as she headed back toward the kitchen. "Look at him, does it look as though he's missed many meals?"

I wasn't sure how to answer that. He certainly wasn't heavy but he did have that mid-life paunch that my father was fighting. The big difference was that my father didn't hide it behind a suit that looked to be worth much more than my father's whole wardrobe.

"This was always a Sunday tradition in our family. When Ethan's brother Todd was still at home—and their mother and I were still married—the four of us would sit down to breakfast together."

"That's how it is in my family," I said. "We all had breakfast together this morning and . . ." I suddenly realized what I was saying. "Sorry."

"Don't be sorry for having a functional family." He hesitated. "Now it's mainly just me, so I appreciate the company. By the way, it was nice that you called your parents."

I'd made a quick call to tell them that I was over at Ethan's so they would know why I hadn't come back from my "run."

"Well, they worry."

"I think all parents worry about their children," he said. "But I think Ethan actually enjoys worrying me."

"I'm sure he doesn't mean to."

"And I'm sure he doesn't care one way or another. He used to bring his friends home all the time . . . although, technically, he didn't bring you home either. So, what is my son up to these days?"

"School, mainly." What else was I supposed to say?

"And that's why he was out so late and got drunk last night? I assume that's why you ended up driving his car. I guess I should be grateful for that, at least."

"We were out on a double date." I thought it best not to say two double dates. "And he really didn't have that much to drink. I drove as a precaution."

"You don't drink?"

"Not much. I guess I was the designated driver last night."

"How do you know my son?" Mr. Frost said.

"I was new to the school and they assigned Ethan to be my host and show me around."

Mr. Frost laughed. "Only my son could convince them to assign somebody with his record to be a host."

"He's very good at convincing people to do what he wants, and convincing them that they wanted it to begin with," I said.

"That's very well said. He is a born lawyer. I've always hoped that he'll join me and his older brother in the family trade."

"He's never mentioned being a lawyer specifically, but he does talk about university."

"Really?"

"He talks about getting into an Ivy League school."

"He hasn't talked to me about that at all. I guess all those donations I've made will finally pay off. I'd better make some calls."

"I'm sure Ethan would like that."

"It's hard for me to know what he likes and doesn't like these days. Say, I was wondering, and I hope you don't mind, but why are you trying to be a vegetarian? Is it for dietary or religious reasons?"

"More ethical. I've got a friend who's into the whole animal rights movement. She's part of an ongoing protest against the killing of pigs."

"Is she one of the protesters down on Lakeshore?"

"Yes, she is. How do you know about that?" I asked.

"The city isn't that big. I passed them yesterday and I was impressed by their determination, standing out there on that little traffic island in the pouring rain."

"Yeah, I was there for a little while yesterday. I got completely soaked."

"Was Ethan there with you?"

"No, he wasn't." Not only had Ethan not been there, he still didn't know anything about *me* being there. Would his father bring it up? Keeping information from people was getting far more complicated than I liked.

"That's too bad. It would be nice if he were taking an interest in that kind of thing again," Mr. Frost said.

"Did he ever?"

He laughed. "He used to give me such a hard time about some of my corporate clients. I expected he'd become some sort of human rights lawyer. Who knows what he might become? Who knows who he is now? I certainly don't."

I suddenly felt very embarrassed and awkward being there. I focused on the pancakes on my plate.

"I don't even know if he's dating anybody. Is he?"

"Nobody special."

"I'm just glad he isn't living like a monk."

I couldn't stop myself from laughing out loud. "Sorry. It's just . . . there's no danger of that! He goes out. A lot."

"That's good to hear."

I wondered what he'd think if he knew that one of those "dates" was a woman in her thirties. Who knows, they could have been dating the same person . . . No, I remembered Ethan saying his father would never date anybody that "old."

"How well does your father know you?" Mr. Frost asked.

That was such a strange question that I didn't know what to say, but he was looking at me in such a direct way that I got the feeling he wasn't going to let me out of this.

"Pretty well, I guess. I grew up in a small town. It would have been tough to have secrets from anybody there."

"You must be finding the city quite different. Just out of curiosity, were you angry when your family had to move? It couldn't have been easy changing schools in your senior year."

"I wasn't happy," I said. "I was even angry for a while. But it wasn't like it was something that was planned just to screw me up."

"I think Ethan still feels that way about our divorce—that it was a personal attack on him," he said.

I shook my head. "He's never said anything like that to me."

"It's sad that you seem to know more about him than I do these days. I should try to do something about that—when I'm back."

"Where are you going?" I asked.

"I'm going away on a ten-day business trip to Tokyo . . . wait . . . do you think he'd like to come along with me?" Mr. Frost asked.

"Japan? For ten days? If he doesn't want to go with you, you can take me instead and I'll pretend to be your son!"

Mr. Frost laughed. "Berta, can you come in here, please?"

She pushed through the door. She was holding a pot of coffee.

"Berta, can you please wake up Sleeping Beauty and tell him I've got a surprise for him? Oh, and by the way, instead of a pay raise, how would you like an extra ten days of holiday, starting this afternoon?"

CHAPTER TWENTY

Ethan was hastily throwing things into a suitcase. "I can't believe it. Ten days in Japan with my father instead of going to school!"

"I think that's the plan."

"I don't know whether I should punch you or hug you for suggesting it," he said.

"It was your father's idea, so I'd actually prefer you did neither."

"Are you sure you don't want to come along?" Ethan asked. "There's an extra seat or five on the corporate jet."

"I appreciate the offer, but I think this is a father-son sort of thing."

"You're a son. Besides, having you along might make it easier. We haven't done much father-and-son stuff for a while. Ten days might be a significant overdose."

"Sorry, but there's no way my parents are going to go for the idea of me flying off to Japan with you and your dad."

"Let my father talk to them. He's pretty good at convincing people to do whatever he wants."

"Like father, like son," I said.

"We're not at all alike. We're very different people!" he snapped.

Obviously I'd hit a sore spot.

"Besides," I pointed out, "even if my parents agreed, I can't afford to miss that much time at school. I have to keep my marks up if I'm going to get into a good college next year. By the way, your father said he was going to make some calls for you about your university."

"You two had quite the breakfast conversation. Is there anything else that you told him that I need to know about?"

"I did mention the criminal charges, and your fascination with small furry animals in a way that most people would consider unhealthy and unnatural and slightly repulsive."

"Those he knew about. After all, he's the one who used to buy me the hamsters and gerbils to begin with. As my shrink would say, he was my enabler," Ethan joked.

"He did tell me some things about you. Why were you giving me such a hard time about being involved with the Social Justice Club at my school? It sounds like you were practically the president of your own chapter."

"We learn, we grow, we evolve, and we change. In a past life it would have been me falling for Veggie-girl instead of you."

"I'm not falling for anybody," I said.

"You keep saying that and maybe you'll start to believe it yourself. You have to be careful of her."

"She's neither armed nor dangerous," I said.

"She's both. Being shot doesn't compare with being heartbroken. Not that I'd know, since I've never been shot."

But obviously he had been heartbroken. That explained so much.

"By the way, thanks for offering to drive us to the airport," he said.

"I'm sure you two could have got there on your own."

"There's a limo service my father uses, but it's nice to be dropped off. Reminds me of the days when my brother, mother, and I would bring him to the airport."

"I guess, really, I should be thanking you for lending me your car. That was unbelievably generous." I still wasn't sure how it was going to fly with my parents.

"How else could you get here to check on the house like you promised?" Ethan asked.

Berta was going to be taking advantage of her ten-day break to visit with family. I'd offered to take in the mail and water the plants.

"Besides, a vehicle like that just *needs* to move," he said. "It gets restless if it isn't used. If it isn't driven, it might sneak out at night and drive itself. You're going to make quite the impression on Veggie-girl when you take her out in my car."

"What makes you think I'm asking her out?"

"Yeah, right. Just try not to do anything stupid in my absence. Remember, speed kills, and I'm not talking about my car now."

After dropping them at the airport, I drove off carefully, aware that they were watching. I started back toward my house, thinking how surprised my parents were going to be. Rather than calling them—and I wouldn't do that while driving anyway—I was going to pull up and show them. My father loved cars, and he'd commented on more than occasion about Ethan's BMW. Maybe if I could convince him to come for a drive with me, he'd be less likely to make me drive it back and park it in the Frosts' driveway.

There was one more thing I wanted to do, just in case.

I pulled to the side of the road and stopped, then took out my phone.

R u interested in getting together? I texted to Raine.

I sat and waited for the reply. It didn't take long.

Doing school stuff but could use short break. What did u have in mind?

Walk, run, bike, balloon ride. U decide. I texted back.

I'm up for a balloon ride, she responded.

That could be a little hard to arrange, but I had an idea.

Will pick up. Address?

She sent back her address. It wasn't far from where I lived, which was both reassuring and troubling: it was an involuntary violation of Ethan's rules about dating too close to home.

I'd have to make one quick stop before I picked her up.

CHAPTER TWENTY-ONE

I was, to say the least, a little nervous as I stood on the doorstep of her house. It was nice, about the same vintage and similar style to our new home. I knocked, and she answered almost immediately. And she burst into laughter.

"Am I that funny-looking?" I asked.

"When you said balloon ride I had no idea what you meant."

Tied to my left wrist were two red, helium-filled balloons. "I don't know if we have quite enough balloons for liftoff, but we could try. You ready to go?"

"For sure." She turned and yelled back into the house. "I'll be home soon. I've got my phone."

She took my hand and tried to lead me away. I stood my ground.

"Don't you want me to meet your parents?"

"I want to go for a coffee."

"You know, parents generally love me."

"What makes you think those were my parents in there?" she asked.

"I guess it could have been your boyfriend or your husband you were yelling goodbye to," I said.

"It was my husband *and* my boyfriend. That's why I'm leaving. They can be so annoyingly jealous when I bring home another other guy."

"Then I guess we really should be going." Still holding hands, we walked toward Ethan's car and I pulled open the passenger door.

"This is Orion's car, isn't it?" she asked.

"Yeah. I wish it were mine though." It did look amazing, sun glistening off the red paint and chrome, the top down so it looked even sweeter. This was a car that looked like it was going fast even when it was standing still.

"This car seems just like the type he'd drive . . . wait . . . he's not coming with us, is he?"

"Of course not."

"Good!"

Even if it made me feel a bit disloyal, I kind of liked her not liking him.

"He's away with his father on a trip. He said I could drive it while he's gone."

She climbed in, and I circled around and sat down behind the wheel.

"Before we start, there's one thing I need to do." I untied one of the balloons from my wrist and tied it onto Raine's. "Could you also put on your seatbelt? I don't want you to float away."

I started it and revved the engine slightly to hear the power. Carefully I pulled away. As I picked up speed, the two balloons fluttered behind us.

"I guess it was nice of him to lend you his car," Raine said.

"He's a nice guy."

"Emma's been waiting for him to call."

"Let her know that he's gone to Japan for ten days. His dad invited him at the last minute, so he didn't know."

"And will he call when he gets back?" she asked.

"I don't know . . . he might."

"It would probably be better if he didn't," she said. "He doesn't strike me as somebody interested in a relationship."

"Maybe he's just waiting to find the right person. Isn't that what we're all trying to do?" I asked.

"Some are trying harder than others would be my guess."

"Hard to argue with that." I quickly changed the subject. I didn't want talk about Ethan to spoil our date. "So, I was thinking we could go down to the lake for a walk, or, I guess, a very low-flying balloon ride."

"That would be nice. And I'm glad we won't be too far off the ground, because I'm actually afraid of heights," she said.

"We're all afraid of something."

"What are you afraid of?" Raine asked.

"Getting hurt," I said, the words flowing out before I thought not to say them.

"Have you been hurt before?" she asked.

I almost blurted out the answer, but I stopped myself. It wasn't necessary, and if nothing else, it would make me sound pathetic. Who would want to date pathetic? Pathetic people became nails.

"You've probably never fallen from a high place, but you're still afraid of them," I said. "I've never been bitten by a snake, but I'm still unnerved by them."

"That's good information. Now I'll be careful not to involve any of my pet snakes in our dates," she said.

"So . . . you admit that this is a date?"

"I'm only willing to admit it's a balloon ride," she joked.

I pulled the car into the parking lot for the walking path and turned immediately into one of the open spots.

"How about if we make a deal," I said. "Let's go for a balloon ride on a semi-date. Deal?"

"Deal," she said.

We joined in with a throng of people using the path—there were old people, families pulling wagons, young adults running and walking and boarding and biking. We bobbed through the crowd, balloons tied to our wrists identifying us as being together. There was another common theme, though—everybody seemed happy, seemed to be enjoying the bright afternoon sun. That was how I felt. I was happy to be there, and even happier to be there with Raine.

"So, since you wouldn't let me meet them, can you at least tell me more about your family?" I said.

"You know, Dakota, you're a little different," Raine said.

"Different can be good."

"In this case it is. Most guys seem to want to just talk about themselves. You keep asking me questions."

That was partly who I was and partly thanks to a tip that Ethan had taught me. Not only did girls like being asked questions, but giving away less information about your pretend-self left less room for mistakes to be made.

"My parents have been asking me questions about you and I realized I don't know that much. I don't even know your last name," she said.

"Well, it could be a problem for a vegetarian. My last name is Fox."

"I like animals. Especially the clever ones."

"What's your last name?"

"Barkowski."

"Thank goodness," I said. "That is such a relief."

She looked confused.

"I'm just so happy it isn't Barrel, or Spout, or Dance. If you were Raine Dance that would be so sad. It would probably mean the end of our time together."

"Somebody seems to think he's very clever."

"Clever like a fox."

"Keep in mind that there's probably an inverse relation between how cute you really *are* and how clever you *think* you are," she said.

"I'm glad to hear that Raine Barkowski thinks I'm cute."

"You're just lucky that I'm too mature to make fun of your name, Dakota," she said.

"Are you going to call me another state?" I asked. "Rhode Island, or perhaps New York?"

"You know, I could make fun of your last name, Fox. What if your first name was something different, like Red?"

"There was a comedian once called Redd Foxx. If I had red hair, that might even have been my nickname."

"Well, how about . . . um . . . Bushytail?"

"If my parents had named me Bushytail, I'd expect to be made fun of. Regardless, it's very nice to meet you, Raine Barkowski."

I offered my hand and we shook. I tried to let go but she held on.

"I'm holding on to you until you answer some more questions," she said.

"Then that settles it. I'm never going to answer any questions for the rest of my life. You're not very good at this whole manipulation thing, are you?"

"Not one of my strengths. But could you please tell me about yourself?" she asked. "Please?"

"How could I turn down somebody as polite and persistent as Raine Barkowski? Have you ever heard of Twenty Questions?" I asked.

"Of course. I've played it."

"Good game, but the problem is there are too many questions. I'll answer ten questions about me if you'll answer one question about yourself. Is that a deal?" I asked.

The words came out too quickly to stop. How was I going to remember that many lies? No, wait, I wasn't going to tell her lies. Lies would be hard to keep track of, but I'd only tell her the truth about me. I wanted her to know who she was dating, even if she didn't know my real first name.

"That's a good deal," she said

"In fact, I'll make that deal with you for every single time we go out on a date," I added.

"That's pretty presumptuous on your part, assuming there will be any more dates after this so-called balloon ride."

"I'll take that chance. I'm betting your curiosity will trump your obvious aversion to me."

We walked over to a picnic table, and I slid into one side while she took a seat on the other. We held hands across the table.

"Ask away," I said.

"Who's in your family?" she asked.

"I have a younger sister named Olivia, and my dad is an accountant, and my mom is a teacher. Next question."

"What school do you go to?"

"Ridgeway. Senior year, but you knew that already, didn't you?"

"Yeah, come to think of it, I did."

"You're obviously not fully valuing these questions. Number three."

"Where do you live?"

"I live at 170 . . . I mean, 16 Hepburn."

"You aren't sure about where you live?" Raine asked.

"I started to give you my old address, 170 Chambers Avenue. That's the one that's been in my head, been my answer for my whole life, so it's hard to think of anything else. I now live at 16 Hepburn."

"I know that street. I have a friend who used to live there."

I was very glad she used the past tense.

"Was it hard to move away from where you'd always lived?" she asked.

"Is that question number four or just a random question?" I asked.

"Question four."

"About the hardest thing I ever did in my entire life, and maybe the best thing, too."

"Why the best thing?"

"Again, is this a formal question, number five?"

"Yes."

"If I hadn't moved, I wouldn't have met a very special person . . . somebody who I love being around . . . Orion."

She reached out with her other hand and smacked me in the shoulder.

"Oh, and I met you, too. Question number six."

"What's the name of the first person you kissed?"

"If I said you, would you believe me?" I asked.

"No. Who was it?"

"I can't really remember her name."

"Were you drunk at the time?" she asked, incredulous.

"I certainly hope not. I was ten years old. It was at a party, and as part of a game I had to go into a closet with a girl for sixty seconds."

"That was you?" she asked.

"Very funny! No, it wasn't you. I would have remembered kissing somebody named Raine. I think it was Sharon or Karen, or something like that."

"And you didn't think to ask her for her name after you kissed?"

"I was told her name earlier, and it gets a little awkward to ask for somebody's name after you've kissed them. How about you, who was the lucky guy you gave your first kiss to?"

"If I said you, would you believe *me*?" she asked.

"I'd believe whatever you told me, absolutely."

"So is that your question to me?" she asked.

I shook my head. "No, I don't think so. I'm much more concerned about who you're going to kiss next."

She blushed and looked down slightly at the table.

"Could I have my hand back for a second?" I asked.

Very deliberately I held my hand up and then wiped it on the sleeve of my shirt. "One of us is sweating, and I suspect it might be me." I took her hand, wiped it on my sleeve, and then held it again. "Go on. Next question, number seven."

"How many girlfriends have you had?"

"Are we counting imaginary ones?"

"Real ones."

"That severely limits the number. Can I say that I'm working on my second real girlfriend as we speak? You'd like her, a little opinionated, and the strangest first name, but I think she's worth the trouble."

She gave me another poke in the arm.

"Although her tendency toward violence goes completely against what I'd expect from a vegetarian. Imagine hitting an innocent, defenceless Fox."

"Not so defenceless, and probably not that innocent. So you're telling me that you've only had one girlfriend before this? And I'd like to point out that this is simply a clarification of question seven."

"It lasted a long time. Most of high school."

"Did it end because you had to move away?" Raine asked.

"To answer question eight, I think that was part of why it ended, but it was headed for the end before the move."

"Was it your idea or hers?" Raine asked.

"I'm supposed to say it was mutual."

"But it wasn't?"

I found myself suddenly lost in what I was supposed to say. Ethan would have told me not to reveal that I'd been hammered, that I'd been the one who lost. But that was a lie, and I was determined to tell her the truth, even if it hurt, and worse, even if it hurt my chances with her.

"I didn't see it coming. Any more than I saw her starting to date my best friend. You'd think they could have at least waited until I moved away, but they didn't." I paused. "Last question."

"Does it still hurt?"

I let out a big sigh. "Not as much as it did yesterday, and more than it's going to hurt tomorrow. I'm starting to think it was for the best. Now, my turn. Are you ready for your question?"

"I'm ready. Go ahead."

"Okay. What's the most important thing you're looking for in a boyfriend?"

"That's easy. Honesty."

I smiled, though I felt it as a stab to the heart. It was the one thing I couldn't entirely give her.

"Look, that's so sweet," Raine said, glancing over my shoulder.

I turned to see. There was an elderly couple, the woman in a wheelchair, and they were feeding the ducks at the shoreline. They were both smiling and laughing, and she reached up and gave his hand a squeeze.

"How long do you think they've been together?" she asked.

"I'm figuring it's at least their second or third date."

"I guess there's only one way to find out," Raine said.

She got up and went over to the couple while I stayed seated at the picnic table. She spoke with them, but I couldn't hear the conversation. What I could see was more smiles and laughter. I was tempted to go over but I was enjoying just watching.

Raine took the balloon from her wrist and tied it to the arm of the wheelchair. The woman clapped her hands, and then Raine leaned down and gave her a big hug. She started back, with a smile bigger than the balloon. The woman and man waved to me, and I waved back.

There was now one more thing for me to add to that list of what I liked about her.

CHAPTER TWENTY-TWO

"Okay, I'm ready for question seventy-six," I said.

"Let me think about it a little bit more," Raine said.

"Are you running out of questions?"

"You'd better hope not. I'm only dating you for the answers."

"Have you ever thought that maybe I'm only dating you for the questions?" I asked.

She reached up, wrapped her arms around me, and gave me a kiss. "I hope you're interested in more than just my questions."

"That would be telling. So, I'm waiting for your next question."

Over the past week and a half we'd been out seven more times. We'd gone to dinner twice, a movie, coffee, another protest at Pig Island followed by a coffee, a house party thrown by a friend of hers, and for another walk—this time without balloons to help. Each time she had been allowed her ten questions. She had asked me about things that I'd never even thought about. It felt as though it wasn't just her getting to know about me, but me getting to know myself. It had been so intense and so fun, but at the same time, it felt, well, dangerous.

Ethan was still in Japan, but I knew what he would have to say about all of this, all of his concerns. I had the same thoughts in my head. What had I got myself into? I should have slowed things down. I should have stopped, but I couldn't. I was powerless. What was the way forward now? How would I tell a girl who lived a life filled with honesty and integrity, who always seemed to do the right thing, that she didn't even know the name of the person she'd been dating?

I'd tried to think it through. Maybe I could tell her that my second name was Dakota but my friends back home called me Graham, my real name. I'd even thought about telling my parents that I wanted to be known as Dakota from this point on, and then I'd legally change my birth certificate. That was stupid. And desperate. And I was both of those. And this girl was neither.

How did I tell a girl who was a devoted vegetarian that hamburger was one of my favourite things in the world? It was small consolation that I hadn't eaten any pork. It wasn't just the pigs, but also because of Raine. The cause was so important to her, and that made it important to me. I couldn't eat pork without feeling that I was cheating on her. No matter what happened, I was sure that I was never going to eat another piece of bacon, another piece of pork, for the rest of my life.

The longer I waited, the bigger my deception was growing, and the harder it was going to be to climb back out of the hole I was digging.

"Question seventy-seven. What's the most romantic thing you've ever done?"

"Afraid I can't tell you that."

"You have no choice. You promised to answer!" she protested.

"But if I do it could potentially ruin our next date."

"Very slick. Okay, I'll let you away with that one for now. Question seventy-eight. Do you want to meet my parents?"

That one caught me by surprise. "Yes, of course I do."

"That's good, because they really want to meet this mysterious person who's been taking me out. My brother thinks I've made you up. When do you want to meet them?"

"In answer to question seventy-nine, whenever you want."

"Hey, that wasn't a question!" she protested.

"By any definition of what constitutes a question, asking me 'when' is certainly a question. You have one more. Go ahead."

"Would you like me to meet your family?" she asked.

"I'd like that, and so would they. Your parents aren't the only ones who have been asking a lot of questions."

But how was this going to be possible? Could I convince my parents to play along with my name, with me being vegetarian? Would they do that? Would

THE ART OF PICKING UP GIRLS

Olivia do that? It would be asking them to lie. And first, I'd have to admit to them what I'd been doing. They'd be disappointed in me—maybe even more than I was disappointed in me.

"So when will that happen?" she asked.

"Oh, I'm so sorry, but that's the end of the questions for today's segment!" I needed more time to think this through.

"Sometimes you drive me crazy!" she exclaimed.

"So it's only sometimes that I'm a disappointment?" I looked at my watch. "I've got to get going. Do you want me to drop you off or do you want to come to the airport?"

"Just drop me off. I wouldn't want to interfere with the serious bro-love between you and Orion. I'm going to miss his car though."

"You could always date Orion instead," I pointed out.

"You got me. I was only dating you for the car, because that's the sort of person I am. Your time is almost up. So before I dump you for the guy with the cool ride, what would you like to know about me?"

"I'm going to save this question and put in the bank like the last two. Just remember, three questions are still mine to ask."

"I'll remember."

"You'd better, because a deal is a deal. Do you want to meet me at Clever Bunny this evening or should I pick you up at your place?"

"I thought you had to give back the car," Raine said.

"My parents will let me use the minivan."

228

"I guess if I come we'll definitely know that I wasn't dating you for your car. Tell you what, I'll meet you there."

I pulled up to the terminal for international arrivals. Ethan had texted to say the plane had landed and we'd agreed where we'd meet. I turned off the engine and felt a little twinge of remorse. That was the last time I was going to be turning this car off. The last drive I was going to have.

I saw Ethan before he saw me. He was towing his bag behind him. I didn't see his father, though. I hit the trunk release and jumped out to wave and caught his attention. He came toward me, his stride short, his shoulders slightly hunched. He looked tired. How long had the flight been and how many time zones had he been through?

"Hey, brother, how you doing?" I called out.

"Tired. Very tired."

I took his bag and threw it in the trunk. "Where's your father?"

"Somewhere in Tokyo. He didn't come back with me."

"That's too bad."

"Business didn't conclude, so he had to stay. It made for a quieter flight," Ethan said.

I went to hand him the keys to the car.

"I think it's better for both of us if you drive. There's a big chance that I'm going to fall asleep on the way home."

He climbed into the passenger seat and I climbed in behind the wheel. At least I had one more drive with his car.

"So, how was Japan?" I asked.

"It has some very fine hotels, and cable news networks to keep me informed of world events."

"You must have done something other than watch TV."

"Obviously I ate, or I wouldn't have survived. The food is good, although given the invention of both fire and utensils, you'd think that they could provide more cooked food and a more efficient way to eat it."

"But you and your father did some other things together, didn't you?"

"A couple of things, but he was pretty occupied with his business, not to mention a few hot dates, so our time was limited."

"But I thought he was bringing you along to spend time with you."

"You obviously don't know him very well . . . which is probably fortunate for you. What my father says and what he does are very different things. But no worries. I'd hoped for more, but somehow it's better that he's at least predictable," Ethan said. "Look, I got out of eight days of school so it wasn't like it was a complete waste. I'm going to go home and have a nap. I was thinking we could hit one of the clubs tonight."

"I thought you were tired."

"I'll grab a few Zs, and then nighttime is actually more like daytime for me right now. Why, do you have something else happening?"

"I sort of have some plans."

"Sort of, or do?"

"I do."

"Do your plans involve a certain vegetarian girl?"

I nodded. "I've been spending a lot of time with Raine."

"And what does she think about you being named Graham instead of Dakota, and the fact that Graham's not really a vegetarian?"

"Nothing yet."

"As in, she doesn't know?"

"Not yet," I admitted.

"And when she finds out, how do you think she's going to react?"

"I'm hoping she'll understand," I said.

"And do you think she will . . . really?"

I shook my head. "Hope is all I've got. Do you have any ideas?"

"You know, the longer this goes on the more it's going to hurt."

"I think that's why I keep putting it off. It's not just that I can't find the words, I just want it to last a little bit longer . . . and longer . . ."

"You know this can only end badly. The only question is just how badly."

That wasn't what I wanted to hear but I didn't think I could disagree.

"I kept thinking that maybe you'd have a solution," I said. "Somehow, if anybody could figure a way out of this, I thought it would be you."

"Nice compliment, and I do have a solution, but I don't think you're going to like it," he said.

I was pretty sure I knew what his solution was.

"It's like a bandage on a scab. You can't take it off slowly. You just have to yank it off all at once. It's the only way that makes sense. Now, if you don't mind, I'm going to close my eyes. I really need to get some sleep."

CHAPTER TWENTY-THREE

I looked at my watch again. It wasn't like Raine to be late, and she was getting later by the moment. I reached for my phone to text her, but stopped myself. I didn't want to appear to be bugging her. She'd be here soon, I was sure.

I signalled for another refill on my coffee. I didn't need to tell them what I wanted because I was almost a regular. It was a strange, funky little restaurant, the Clever Bunny, but it had come to feel like my place. More important, it was beginning to feel like *our* place.

I'd spent a lot of time thinking over what Ethan had said. On one hand, he was right. The longer the lying went on, the harder it was going to be to come clean. I knew that already. I also knew that it was all or nothing. I could maybe make a lie into the truth by really becoming a vegetarian, but I couldn't become Dakota.

In some ways, Raine being late was helpful. It was giving me more time to think. Maybe tonight would be the night I told her the truth. I'd gone over it a dozen times, trying to figure out the right way—easing into it, little by little, or just blurting it straight out. In the end, I had to agree with Ethan—it was like removing a bandage. One clean, fast pull would be the only way to do it. This was going to hurt. Even if it went well, it would cause pain. It might be the end of our relationship, but this time I'd know exactly what I'd done wrong. It really would be my fault, and she'd have every reason to break it off. And at least I could be guaranteed that my ex-girlfriend wouldn't start to date my best friend.

But I couldn't assume the worst. I had to hope instead it would be a new beginning. One based on trust and truth and honesty.

I thought about Elmer and Jennifer. I'd been so distracted by Raine, I hadn't really given much thought to what Olivia had discovered on Facebook. I wondered who had broken it off, whose idea it was. I think I would have liked it if it was Elmer—that he felt so bad about what he'd done to me that he'd ended it.

There was a candle on the table in the little booth at the back that they'd set aside for us. It had become "our table." It was as close to a private spot as the restaurant had, and this was as close as I could come to a romantic date—the answer to the question I hadn't answered.

I'd already ordered for both of us—a little presumptuous, but the owners, Ted and Barb, who were such nice people, had helped me to select all of her favourite things. I pictured wilting lettuce leaves in the kitchen of the restaurant waiting for her arrival.

Ted and Barb had come over now and again to chat with me, along with the hostess and the waitress, who had both refreshed my water. At first I thought they were just being friendly. After awhile, though, I suspected that they were checking up on me. I was starting to feel very much alone, and while it was pretty dark in our little corner, I felt as though there was a bright light being shone on me. It reminded me of sitting alone in the cafeteria on my first day at the new school. Ethan had rescued me there. I needed Raine to come, soon, and do the same.

I looked at my watch again. She was now forty-five minutes late. I went over the invitation in my head. There was no way that either of us had got the time wrong . . . or was there? I'd just send her a friendly text. Maybe she was sitting at home, waiting for me to pick her up, equally confused.

We were meeting here, right? I typed. Was that rude? No, just clear.

I'd just wait and—there was a reply.

I won't be coming.

I typed back. **Why? Is something wrong?**

An instant reply. **You. You're what's wrong, Graham.**

What did that mean? I was what was wrong? And then I finally saw it: "Graham." I stared at my name— my *real* name—on the screen, feeling as though I'd been kicked in the gut.

I can explain, I typed with shaking hands.

No you can't, she replied.
Just meet me. Talk to me. Please.
No. I can't do that.

Was that it? Was it over? Were these few little typed words going to be it? I had to see her, at least try to explain. There was one thing I could try.

U still owe me 3 questions.
You owed me the truth.

I did. I do. Regardless—3 questions. Keep your word. I'll meet you in front of your house.

I looked the words over carefully. A few words, five short sentences. I sent the text and waited.

I felt numb all over. What was she going to say? Was she even going to reply at all, or was that it?

I'll be waiting, came the reply.

I pulled the minivan up to the curb. I could see her in the shadows, sitting on the edge of the porch. I turned off the engine and took a deep breath. There was pressure in my chest, my stomach was uneasy, and I felt like I was going to be sick. I took a second and third deep breath. I couldn't just sit there. If I'd seen her, I knew that she'd seen me pull up. It was time.

I got to the path, and she was there at the end. Sitting stone-still, head down, her arms wrapped around her legs. I expected her to look up as I approached but she didn't.

"Hello, Raine," I said softly.

She looked up but didn't answer. Somehow I'd hoped her eyes would be fiery, that her expression would be angry. Instead she just looked sad, and it was obvious that she'd been crying. The little makeup she wore had run slightly down her cheeks. I went from feeling bad to suddenly feeling worse. My stomach hurt, and it was like I'd been struck but I'd also been the one who threw the punch.

"I'm so sorry," I said.

"So am I," she replied, her voice barely louder than a whisper.

"If we could just talk."

She shook her head. "Three questions. That's all."

In the rush to get there I hadn't even thought of what the questions would be. Now I had to come up with three. Three perfect questions. They were my last hope. My only hope.

"Question one." I hesitated while I tried to think it through. "Is there anything I can say or do to change your mind?"

"No."

I'd hoped for something more. Even if it was just her saying no to me but with more words. Something I could build on. I took another deep breath and strained to figure out the next question.

"Okay, second question. I know how you're feeling, I understand how you're feeling right now, but do you think you could ever forgive me?"

This time she just shook her head, and I felt an ache in my heart. I stood there, speechless, staring, unsure of what to say next, what to do next.

"One more question," Raine said. "You have one more question and then you have to leave."

I had the question in my head now, but I was afraid of what the answer was going to be. Even worse, I was almost sure what the answer was going to be.

"Do you want me to leave you alone? Not call or text you ever again?"

For the first time she looked right at me, right into my eyes, right into my heart.

"Don't ever contact me again."

I felt my lower lip start to quiver. I knew the tears weren't far away, and I could see them starting to form in her eyes. That hurt even more.

"Why didn't you tell me?" she asked. I could hear the tears, the hurt in her voice.

"I wanted to. I tried. I was going to try again tonight. I was just afraid."

"Afraid of what?" she asked.

"Of what's happening right now, that it would mean the end."

She laughed. A sad laugh that caught me by surprise. "I guess you were right. It does mean the end."

"You know, all those questions you asked me, all eighty questions. I answered them truthfully. I told you things I've never told anybody."

"You needed to tell me your name."

"It was just a game. A stupid game—that's how it started—and then I couldn't stop," I tried to explain. "It was my way of trying not to get hurt. I was wrong, but it doesn't matter. I deserved to get hurt. I still deserve to be hurt. You deserve nothing but happiness. I guess 'sorry' doesn't mean much coming from a liar."

She didn't reply. She was fighting to hold back the same tears I was fighting.

"I can't make it up, and I deserve what I'm getting. I'm so sorry that I hurt you. But I'll do what you asked and I'll leave you alone. I just want you to know that I know what I've lost. Goodbye, Raine Barkowski."

I turned, took a step, and stumbled down the path. I heard her crying and wanted to turn back, to make her feel better, to take away her pain. But I couldn't. I was the one who had caused it. I continued down the path and away.

CHAPTER TWENTY-FOUR

When a car honked at me I waved a weak apology—
another one that didn't mean much—and pulled
over to the side of the road. I wasn't sure what I'd
done to annoy another driver, but I knew my mind
wasn't on the road. I'd driven away with no destination in mind. Now I wasn't sure how I'd got here, or
where exactly I was, or how badly I was driving. I
needed to get back into my head and mentally
behind the wheel before I got back on the road
again. I turned the minivan off and pulled the keys
out of the ignition.

What now? I needed to talk to somebody, but
it couldn't be my parents. They'd be mad at her for
breaking it off with me, and I couldn't tell them whose
fault it really was, what I'd done, because then they'd
be disappointed in me. I was already disappointed

enough in me for everybody. I felt almost as embarrassed as I did heartbroken.

If only this hadn't happened, if only she hadn't found out . . . how had she found out? Even in a city this big, I supposed, it was hard for a secret to not come to light. Didn't she say she had a friend who lived on my street? No, wait, a friend who used to live on my street. That couldn't be it. But she did know my address—I'd told it to her. What if she'd knocked on the door and asked for Dakota, and my parents had told her there was no Dakota there but there was a Graham? That would mean that they already knew what I'd done . . . if that was what had really happened. I had no way of knowing.

I needed to talk to somebody. There were only two people I could talk to—and I'd just promised one of them, the one who could help me the most, that I'd never contact her again. The only person left was Ethan. I could call him—no, I needed to talk face to face. I'd drive over and hope that he was home.

With a goal in mind I felt more composed. I was ready to drive again.

Funny, but I wasn't just thinking about Raine. I was also thinking about Jennifer, and it was like those old wounds had been opened up again. I was grieving for this relationship, but there was still an echo of what had happened before.

Was that how life worked? Did we ever get over anything, or did we just keep carrying everything around with us? Was that what wore people down, the burden of what had gone wrong in their lives, adding on and adding up until they collapsed under the accumulated weight of it all, all the regrets, all the bad decisions, all the sadness?

I remembered Ethan asking me whether I ever wanted to feel these feelings again. And now I was, except it was worse, harder, deeper, stronger, and even more painful than before. How could that be? I'd only known Raine one month minus a day, and this seemed to hurt more than the end of years of being together with Jennifer.

I pulled into Ethan's driveway. His car was there. So far, so good. I rang the bell, and almost instantly Berta answered.

"Hello, Graham, it's good to see you!" she sang out.

"Hi, Berta. I need to see Ethan."

"Come, he is in the kitchen. I was fixing him supper. I can fix you something too if you're hungry."

"No, but thanks for the offer."

I hadn't had anything except some gluten-free bread sticks but I just didn't feel like eating. It was probably better to keep my stomach empty.

"Hey, buddy, good to see you!" Ethan exclaimed as I entered. "Did you change your mind? Are you coming out with me?"

"No, that's not it."

He looked at me—no, he stared at me. "I was going to ask you how you're doing, but judging from your expression it looks like somebody killed your dog, and I know you haven't got a dog."

"It's worse. Much worse."

"That can only mean one thing. Veggie-girl?"

I nodded.

"She knows everything, and it didn't go well," he guessed.

"She ended it. She never wants to see me again."

"You knew it was going to end badly. There really wasn't any other way, was there?"

"I guess I had hope."

"Hope is never good."

"I guess that sometimes false hope is better than cold reality," I said.

"That's pretty philosophical, but you have to remember that hope is mostly just a trick, an illusion that makes the inevitable fall harder. At least it's over now."

I thought about that and knew he was right. I felt devastated.

"At least in a city this big it's not like you're going to run into her every day."

"That's one plus, I guess."

"A *big* plus. That's why I have that rule about not dating anybody at our school. A rule I'm glad you've been smart enough to follow."

"Is there a rule about never dating anybody ever again?"

"No, but you know my theory: the best way to get over one girl is to find a better girl."

"I remember." How could I forget him saying that the first time we met? How could I explain to him that I didn't think there was a better girl? "But I'm not going out tonight."

"I get it. Oh hey, here's another good thing—you're

not likely to run into any other girl with the same name. You'll only hear it if you tune in to the weather report."

"I don't . . . oh, yeah, I get it."

"I think you really need to let the healing start tonight. Come on out with me."

I just shook my head.

"The Frostman is seldom wrong. I'll make a call and ask my date to scramble a friend for you for the night. We'll have a double date and I'll try to figure out how to make it extra special, and—"

"I'd just be miserable."

"You're going to be miserable whether you stay in or go out, so you might as well go out. Isn't it better not to be alone? Isn't being alone what's causing that pain right now?"

"I guess, but I don't think I can pull that off tonight."

"Okay, I understand, but I still don't think you should be on your own. I'll call my date and tell her I can't make it, and you and I can just hang tonight. Would that help?"

I nodded.

"Don't worry. It will pass. You're just lucky she found out."

"I don't feel so lucky . . . Wait, I didn't tell you she *found out*. I just told you she ended it."

"I just assumed that she found out, that's all."

"But it could have been because I told her. I told you I was thinking about telling her everything. It could have been that," I said.

"You weren't going to be able to do that," he said. "Not for a long time."

I looked at Ethan. I had a terrible thought, but I knew him well enough to know he could fool me if he wanted to. He could lie to somebody and look them straight in the eye and they'd believe him. He could fool me now like he fooled most people. I needed the truth.

"Did you tell her?"

"Why would you—?"

"Just tell me. All I want is the truth. I owed it to her and you owe it to me."

Ethan turned to Berta. "Could you leave us alone for a few minutes, please?"

She nodded and was gone.

"I guess I already know the answer. Why did you do it?" I asked.

"I did it for your own good."

"How is breaking my heart for my own good?"

"I was just trying to save you from more pain," he said.

"I don't know if I could feel more pain than this."

"Yes, you could. A week from now would have been harder. A month from now would have been even harder, more painful for you."

I didn't know what to say. Even if what he was saying was right, that he'd done it for me, it still wasn't his decision to make.

"There was no other way for this to end. I didn't do it to hurt you, but to try to save you from more hurt."

"You had no right."

"I thought a lot about it. If you think I was wrong, then I was wrong. If you want to, you can take a swing at me. I'll understand."

"I don't want to punch you." I suddenly felt a surge of anger. "No, maybe I do." I jumped to my feet, ready and willing to take a swing.

Ethan didn't move or react at all. He just sat there, arms on the table, hands open, not ready to fight, not even preparing to defend himself.

"Go ahead. I won't fight back. It might even make you feel better," he said.

I knew right away it wouldn't help. I lowered my arms, unclenched my hands, and then lowered myself back into the seat.

"Even if it wouldn't make you feel any better, getting punched might make me feel better," he said. "I guess I shouldn't have done it, but you have to believe that I did it for you."

"And not just because you wanted your wingman back?" I asked.

"I can get another wingman. This was about friendship."

Slowly I got up, and as I did I let out a big, deep sigh that caused my whole body to shudder. "I have to go. I have to go home." I took a few steps and turned around. "Could I ask you one question?"

"Of course, you can ask me anything," Ethan said.

"Do you remember when we first met, and you asked me what was the name of the girl who hurt me?" I asked.

He nodded.

"I need to know the same thing. What was her name?"

He stared at me without saying a word.

"The girl, the one who did this to you, the one who hurt you so badly that you can never risk your heart again. What was her name?"

He looked down at the table for such a long time that I didn't think he was going to answer.

"Tracey," he said at last, his voice barely a whisper.

"Does it still hurt?"

"Some days more than others. Today, well, a lot," he said. "Seeing you right now in such pain brings back memories and feelings. I'm so sorry that I did this to you."

"How long were you with her?" I asked.

"That's the funny part, it wasn't long. Just over a month . . . thirty-five days."

"You know the number of days?"

He nodded. "How many days did you know Raine?"

"Thirty."

"I know the date I met her and the date I never saw her again. Some things you don't forget, no matter how hard you try," he said.

"You might be wrong," I said.

"No, I'm not. I thought she was the one."

"I thought you didn't believe in *the one*."

"I don't now, but I did then. She was *special*." He sighed deeply, and I thought I saw the start of tears.

"She must have been really special to hurt you that badly."

"Worse than I could ever imagine possible," he said.

"I know how you're feeling. I wish I didn't," I said. "I'd better get going."

I stood up and reached across the table. He looked surprised, a little confused, but then he extended his hand and we shook.

"Thank you . . . for everything," I said.

"Everything?"

"Yes, everything." I turned and walked away.

CHAPTER TWENTY-FIVE

I grabbed my backpack, closed my locker, and locked it. It had been a hard day, a long day. I just wanted it to end, for the week to end. One more day until Christmas break. I didn't know how I felt about Christmas, but I knew I needed a break. From school. From everyone. From everything.

I'd had a lot of trouble focusing on school since breaking up with Raine. I'd started taking my lunch to the library sometimes and working on assignments while I ate. I tried to convince myself that it was because I had so much to do, but really, I hadn't been doing much work there, either. My mind was just too preoccupied and my feelings were too raw. I wanted to be alone. I didn't want to sit with anybody and pretend to be happy, as if nothing had happened. Besides, I didn't think I could pull that off. I wasn't that good an actor.

Part of me was still angry or upset or confused about Ethan and what he'd done. I could believe that he'd told Raine for my own good, that his intentions were good. But still, what he'd done was wrong. There was no way he should have asked Emma for Raine's number and called her up and told her everything. There was no question about that. But he really was trying to be a good friend—he believed he was throwing himself on yet another grenade, and he was willing to risk our friendship to do it. Still, I was feeling just enough doubt or resentment or whatever that it was uncomfortable to hang out with him. Maybe it was just that being around him reminded me of her, and I didn't need any more reminding.

It all meant that I'd had a lot of time to think in the last couple of weeks. More than I would have liked. I couldn't shut my head off. It was filled with thoughts of Raine, about what could have been, and what I'd lost. Forever.

Walking through the halls, I bumped into people I now knew, exchanged a few words or a simple nod of the head. I ran into the guys going into the gym for basketball practice. They were getting ready for a tournament over the holidays. I missed playing ball. I missed being part of a team. I wondered how many of them knew about Raine breaking it off with me. Probably none. I certainly hadn't told anybody, and I knew Ethan would have kept that to himself. He really had been a loyal friend. *Had* . . . past tense.

Was there any way we could still be friends? Was it over with both my girlfriend and my best friend again?

Was this the same thing in a different way? Instead of Jennifer and Elmer, was it Raine and Ethan?

I stopped dead in my tracks, and somebody bumped into me from behind.

"Sorry," he said.

I looked down—way down. He was a little ninth-grader whose backpack was almost bigger than him. He looked a little bit nervous.

"It's not your fault. I'm the one who should apologize for stopping without warning. Sorry about that."

He looked relieved, gave me a little smile, and moved away.

I walked through the main doors and stopped at the top of the stairs. I scanned the crowd and the driveway, looking for Ethan. I couldn't keep avoiding him. We needed to talk. He and his car weren't hard to find. He was leaning on the hood, waiting in the place where we usually met. There was a little audience surrounding him. As usual, he was holding court. It was as if he was still up on that little stage, performing. He was an actor, and they were an audience watching what he was going to say or do next. I'd been part of that audience, as well as an actor in the play.

He saw me and gave a little wave. I waved back and started down the stairs. By the time I got there the guys had all moved away. It was just Ethan.

"What happened to everybody?" I asked.

"I thought maybe we should talk."

"I was hoping that too. So . . . how are you doing?" I asked.

"I've been better, but the important thing is how are you doing?"

"Still alive. Still here."

"Good to hear. Listen, can I ask *you* a question?" Ethan said.

"You know you can."

"Maybe it isn't even fair for me to ask, but I really want to know: is the second time easier or harder than the first?"

"I wish I could say easier, but it isn't. Right now it feels even harder."

"I was afraid you were going to say that."

"Sorry I don't have a better answer," I said.

"The truth is always best," he said.

"The truth? Um, is that *you* talking?"

He looked at least slightly embarrassed. "I meant with friends. We are still friends, right?"

I shook my head. "You're not just a friend . . . you're a *good* friend."

He looked relieved.

"What you did was wrong. You know that, don't you?"

"Yeah, I do," he agreed.

"But I still think you did it out of friendship."

"You know, I even questioned that myself."

"You did?" I asked.

"Yeah, and I understand you wondering. I didn't want to hurt either of you." He paused. "Raine really did care for you."

"I know. Well, at least she really cared for a guy named Dakota who was a vegetarian and not a liar."

"She liked you. And you may have lied but that doesn't make you a liar."

"No, I'm pretty sure that's the definition of a liar," I said. I wasn't about to let either of us off the hook that easily.

He shook his head. "But you're fundamentally an honest person. A good person."

"Thank you for saying that. You know, you are too."

"Me?"

"You. You, Ethan, are a good person."

"I know hundreds of girls who would disagree," he said.

"Then they're at least partly wrong. What you did and who you are, are two different things. I know who you are, and under all the theories and rules and scams is a good person. You're always there for your friends. Maybe someday you'll be there for a girlfriend. There's more than one special person out there in the world." I'd been thinking about this next part. I took a deep breath. "Just because you were hurt doesn't give you the right to hurt others."

"Don't you remember when I told you it's better to give than—?"

"No, it isn't!" I snapped. "And you know that. Some of your rules are just plain wrong, even if they're right. They cause pain for people who don't deserve it. It's not 'better' if what you've giving is pain and hurt! Do you know the part that's really hard for me right now?"

He shrugged.

"I just wish I hadn't done this to Raine," I said. "That's what hurts so much. Not how I'm feeling but how I made her feel by playing stupid games."

"I guess I can understand that."

"Someday, not yet, I'm going to try again. But not the way we were doing it. Don't you ever get tired of all the games?"

"It's my way of not getting hurt."

"And how is that working out for you?"

"Not great." He paused. "But it doesn't feel as bad as you're feeling."

I didn't see that coming. He was wrong.

"You know, there's only one thing worse than being hurt," I said.

"What's that?"

"Being so afraid of ever getting hurt again that you can't even try to find somebody."

He nodded his head ever so slightly in agreement.

"Not now, but I am going to try again," I told him.

"Even though it would most likely only mean getting hurt again?" he asked.

"You and your rules and theories were right about some things. Odds are whatever relationships I'm in are going to end, and somebody is going to get hurt. And it's probably going to be me at least half the time. I'm willing to take that chance. Not now, not yet, but I will. And, if you like, I'll even take you along with me when I try."

"I guess I'll have to be your wingman on that one."

"How about if it was just two guys trying to figure it out as they go?"

"I don't have a rule for that one."

"How about if we call it the rule of the Blind Leading the Blind?"

He laughed. "I like that one. You know, we could even start that journey with me driving you home," Ethan said.

"On one condition. You need to stay and have dinner with me and my family."

"I don't want to put you out or be a problem."

"How could eating with a friend be a problem? I think my parents miss having you around. I know my sister does! So, will you come for dinner?"

I reached out and offered my hand, and when he took it I pulled him in for a hug. He hugged me back.

CHAPTER TWENTY-SIX

It was nearly a week into the school break, and my parents and sister had gone out for some last-minute Christmas shopping at the mall, leaving me alone in the house. They'd invited me but I'd declined—the same way I'd been declining almost everything that involved leaving the house. I wasn't really in the Christmas spirit. I just wanted to be left alone to play video games and listen to music. The only person I'd talked to outside of my family lately was Ethan. I liked being around him. In spite of everything, he was still one of the funniest, most entertaining people I'd ever met. He'd been over to eat with us twice in the last three days. My parents liked him, and he liked them. I think he really enjoyed being part of our family dinners.

And it wasn't like I was a complete hermit. Ethan and I had gone out a couple of times to grab a coffee and go for a drive. Shockingly, we hadn't even tried to meet any girls. I guess he could have found another wingman, but he hadn't. He wasn't going out as much either . . . although once in a while I saw him almost slipping back into gear, especially when it came to flirting with waitresses. It was hard to break old habits.

The doorbell rang. Whoever it was, it wasn't for me, so I wasn't going to answer it. It was probably somebody selling things door to door, or wanting to convert me to their religion. I ignored it, but it rang a second time. Why didn't they just stop?

When the doorbell rang a third time the person just kept pressing the button. It kept going on and on and on. Whoever it was, they'd picked the wrong guy to annoy. I marched to the door, threw it open, and—

"Hello, sir."

I was stunned. "Raine?"

She pointed to a name tag on her left shoulder. "Yes, that's my name. I'm conducting a survey today, if you'd be willing to answer a few questions." She was holding a pen and a clipboard. "Do you have a few minutes to spare?"

"I can answer anything you want . . . you can have as much time as you want . . . Do you want to come in?"

"No, sir, it's not wise to venture into a stranger's home—no offence."

"None taken. I understand, I guess . . . Why are you here?"

"I'm doing a special, small scale survey. I did mention I was doing a survey, right? Hopefully you can follow along. Before I start with the questions I'm going to need your name—your *full* name."

"Graham Charles Fox."

"Could you spell that, please? I want to make sure I have it correct."

I spelled it out, and she wrote it down on the pad on her clipboard.

"Thank you. It's very important to know the name or the results are invalid. Almost *everything* is invalid if you don't have the right name."

"I guess I agree."

"So, my first question. How long has your family been living here?"

"It's been almost twelve weeks now. Before that, I'd lived where we lived for all of my life."

"The move must have been hard."

"It was difficult, then it was wonderful, the best time I'd ever known. And now, well, it's been unbelievably hard, the worst time I've ever known."

"I'll put down 'very hard,'" she said as she scribbled away. "I think I know what that's like. Next question. Are you a vegetarian?"

"This is certainly a strange survey."

"It's very individualized. So, the answer to my inquiry about your dietary habits?" she asked.

"The last couple of weeks I haven't been eating much of anything, but I do eat some meat. I've been cutting back, and for some reason I just haven't been able to eat any pork products for several weeks now."

"They say pigs are very smart animals," she said.

"In some cases, they are way smarter than certain people. I should point out that I admire people who are vegetarians, and vegans. I'd like to try a little harder to be that way."

"Interesting. I'm a vegetarian," she said.

"I thought you might be, you know, judging from the questions you're asking."

"Next question. Do you have any specific goals in life?" she asked.

"I'm working hard to get into college next year."

"Anything more personal?"

"I'm going to try to be a better person, a more honest person, somebody who deserves to be trusted."

"That's certainly a noble goal. Do you think you can reach it?" she asked.

"All I can do is try my best. It's important to try."

"Now this next question you might find a little strange," she said.

"I've found a lot of these questions strange."

"You're under no obligation to answer. I can leave if you want . . .?"

"No, please don't. Please . . . just go on. I'll answer anything you ask."

"It's very personal."

"You can ask me whatever you want," I said.

"That's good to know. Have you ever hurt anybody?"

I swallowed, and chose my words carefully before I answered. "I have. It was somebody who was very important to me. I regret hurting her so much more than the hurt it caused me." I paused. "Although she

could be stubborn and opinionated and a little sancti-
monious and—"

"I think you'd be wise to simply answer the questions," she said, cutting me off.

"Certainly. Did I mention that she, this person I
hurt, that she was almost perfect?"

"Nobody is perfect."

"She was as close as anybody I've ever met. I
guess she was too good for me."

"Or you were too bad for her." She looked down
at her clipboard, and I couldn't read her expression.
But when she looked up again, her blue eyes were
soft. "Last question. If you had another chance, do
you think you'd ever hurt her, whoever she is, again?"

I knew what I was supposed to say, but that would
have been a lie, and there couldn't be any more lies. I
had to answer truthfully.

"I probably would hurt her again."

She looked shocked.

"And she'll probably hurt me again. Not that I
would ever mean to, and I'd try my best not to, but
we humans, well, we make mistakes. All we can try
to do is fix them."

"And maybe learn to forgive," she said.

She looked directly into my eyes and smiled—a
smile I didn't think I'd ever see again. My heart melted.

"I miss you so much," she said.

"I miss you more than I thought possible."

"Those things you told me, the eighty answers to
the eighty questions—was that you, or Dakota?"

"Me. I don't even know anybody named Dakota."

"Neither do I. That's such a strange name," she said.

"Unlike Raine?" I teased.

She smiled.

"Can I ask you a question?" I said.

She nodded.

"Why did you decide to come here today?"

"Mostly because I missed you."

"Mostly?" I asked.

"That, and Ethan."

"Ethan?" I exclaimed.

"He sat outside my house in his car and told me he wouldn't leave until we talked."

I was shocked. "I didn't know he did that, honestly." He'd managed to keep that a secret from me.

"I know. He told me about you, and how you were feeling, and he told me that it wasn't your fault, and that you deserved another chance."

"I'm surprised you listened to him. I'm surprised you believed him," I said.

"I believed him because it was what I wanted to believe."

"The important thing is that you're here."

"Look, I don't usually do this, ask a person who's practically a stranger . . . you said your name was . . ." She looked down at the clipboard. "Graham, that's it, Graham. I was wondering if you'd be interested in going someplace where we could talk. I think we might have a lot of things in common."

"I'd like that . . . more than anything else in the world."

"We could even have a cup of coffee."

"I could go, but I have one condition," I said.

Her eyes widened in surprise. "What's the condition?"

I reached down and took her hand in mine. "I get to pick the place. I know this café that serves only organic, fair-trade coffee."

She laughed, and those golden flecks danced in her blue eyes. And suddenly, the entire world was right.

ERIC WALTERS is one of Canada's best-known and most prolific writers of fiction for children and young adults. His books have won over 120 awards, including thirteen separate children's choice awards, and have been translated into thirteen languages. He lives in Guelph, Ontario, and is the founder of the Creation of Hope, a charity that provides care for orphans in the Mbooni district of Kenya. In 2014 Eric was named a Member of the Order of Canada "for his contribution as an author of literature for children and young adults whose stories help young readers grapple with complex social issues."

For more information go to www.ericwalters.net.